A simple game of taps has created an undeniable bound between two telegraph operators.

His fear of getting close again erupted along the keys. *If we were face-to-face, I wonder if it would be so easy to say all that we did to one another. Don't make more of this than there is.*

Tears welled and brimmed in her lashes as she tapped out her response. "Why are you doing this? Our lives have not been so different that we can't at least be friends. Really, I'm sorry I said anything about your wife. I won't again, if you prefer it that way."

Friends, Sayra? Is that all you felt pass between us?

His question left her speechless. So much more had taken seed in her heart during the past few days. More than she dared dream possible. But she was afraid to trust those feelings. Afraid the bond that had formed between them might not hold up to the broad light of day, just as he'd said himself, when life could be seen more clearly.

And truth was, the fear that she might disappoint him in some way and a dread that he'd think her wrong in separating Lily from Ulysses prevented her from telling him all.

Can't answer? Stop. That's what I thought. Stop. Badger Springs out.

"Truman, wait! Please. . ." She tapped out message after message, but no reply came. Had he left, or was he sitting there listening, ignoring her plea? Sayra stared at the machine, wishing it could somehow transfer her rather than her words to Badger Springs.

DEWANNA PACE is a multi-published, award-winning author of historical novels. She is also very active in RWA of the Texas Panhandle. *Small Blessings* is her debut with **Heartsong Presents**.

Small
Blessings

DeWanna Pace

Heartsong Presents

This book is dedicated to

THOMAS WAYNE WILLIAMS
"Tommy"

beloved brother and one of
the true heroes in my life,

and to his family

Rose, Jimmy Wayne, Hollie
Camillia, Helena, and Amanda,

precious souls who made
his life worthwhile.

GOD BLESS YOU FOREVER.

A note from the Author:
*I love to hear from my readers! You may write to me at
the following address:* **DeWanna Pace**
Author Relations
P.O. Box 719
Uhrichsville, OH 44683

ISBN 1-55748-930-0

SMALL BLESSINGS

Cover illustration by Jeanne Brandt.

PRINTED IN THE U.S.A.

one

"You must do something about this!" Sayra insisted, grabbing the handle of the butter churn and demanding her older sister to stop and face her. "If you don't, Lily's the one who will suffer."

"Nothing's happened." Bess released the churn and wiped her hands upon her apron.

"Yes, bless the Lord, nothing has happened. But you and I both know, He helps those willing to help themselves. She's pretty and outspoken. A dangerous combination around soldiers who are a long way from home and armed with 'the woman order.' They can mistreat her without even having to think twice about it."

Bess sighed and slumped back into the rocker, raising cornflower blue eyes to meet Sayra's inquiring gaze. Blonde curls had worked loose from her chignon and made her look harried.

"What can I do, Sis? I've talked to Ulysses every night this month about the matter, but he's so frustrated with meeting production demands that he won't admit the truth. He's afraid he can't do anything about it, short of locking her in the house away from everyone. And he won't do that."

Bess wouldn't look at Sayra directly, her voice becoming whisper-soft, "We can't make trouble; you know that. Ulysses says, if we don't want some loyal Northerner to lease our plantation and cotton fields, or

5

if we hope to survive this terrible atrocity everyone's calling reconstruction, then we'd best make certain we produce plenty of cotton to send back east and bury any objections we have along with the next crop." Her reasoning gained momentum with each of the rocker's forward and backward motions. "Lily's just going to have to quit speaking her mind so much, that's all."

"That's like asking the wind to stop blowing," Sayra argued softly, wondering how much longer it would take the nation to forgive itself and heal the wounds of war. Five years had passed, and still true fellowship eluded them. Would this new decade bring real peace? "Lily doesn't know how to lie, Bess. She sees the truth and speaks it. Remember, that's what you taught her . . .you *and* Ulysses. Thou shall not bear false witness."

Sayra wondered what in her sister's marriage had made her so complacent, so ready to allow her husband's inadequacy to act go unchallenged. The two sisters had lived much the same life, had grown up in Port Hudson, Louisiana, with two hard-working parents who'd taught them to respect the teachings of the Bible. . .no matter how difficult that might prove.

"Ulysses might be right, Bess," Sayra admitted, "but that should give us even more reason to search for a way to protect Lily from the order."

"It's so unfair!" Bess rocked harder. "Why did it have to be put back into effect?"

Sayra knew. Men fought the great war, not women. Women had tried desperately to salvage what remained of the nation and to adjust, to heal. To see someone being mistreated now, when all were supposed to be equal, often forced even the gentlest heart to speak its mind.

The federal watchdog who governed Port Hudson with an iron fist chose to call these acts of compassion deliberate abuse and verbal attacks against his soldiers. He had reinstated the "woman order" General Benjamin Butler once put in effect when New Orleans was invaded so that women caught confronting federal soldiers would be treated as soiled doves plying their trade—an order Sayra would see never enforced concerning gentle Lily.

A glance reminded Sayra of her and her elder sister's many differences. At five foot seven, she stood three inches taller than Bess. Where Bess's figure had become plump, her own remained youthfully thin. Instead of having buttercup-colored curls, Sayra's thick tresses looked like a sea of cinnamon, waving almost to her waist when she wore it loose. But the real variance came from the inside. Though both disliked confrontation, each dealt with it in an entirely different manner. Bess ignored conflict and rode out an emotional storm. Sayra acknowledged all the brewing elements and found a way to take the wind out of them. . .which seemed to be the exact approach needed now.

A prayer whispered through her thoughts as she sought an answer to her sister's dilemma. Even before it ended, an idea began to form. "Then why don't you and Ulysses let Lily go with me?" Sayra thanked God for the plan that continued to formulate. "Wasn't he complaining just last Sunday that there were too many mouths to feed around here?"

Bess blushed and stood, moving toward the edge of the porch that ran the length of the homestead. "He didn't really mean to make you feel unwelcome, Sis.

Ulysses is just concerned because prices for seed are so exorbitant lately. He can't just cultivate the crop and send it by rail any more. Now he worries about supplying the sharecroppers' needs, ginning, and all those federal inspections of his warehouses along the wharf. And I'm sure there are countless other worries he doesn't share with me, so I won't worry, too. Besides, you know he promised Mother and Father you could live here until you choose to marry."

Kind of him, Sayra thought, *when the place really should belong to you and I.* For twenty-two years she'd chosen not to marry for convenience or companionship. Sayra wanted to wait on the loving soul God had promised would become her helpmate. Because she waited for the right man, she had been given the title *old maid.* The classification never bothered her until Ulysses made a point of reminding Sayra that his burdens could be eased somewhat if she were to choose one of the beaux who continued to call on her.

Ulysses disapproved of her reason for turning away those who came calling, scoffing at the notion of waiting for love to happen.

"Love will come later," he had insisted and patted Bess's hand affectionately, "won't it, dear?"

The look in Bess's eyes that hadn't quite matched the smile of assurance she'd given her husband encouraged Sayra to stand firm in her conviction. She would not marry until the Lord laid it upon her heart that she'd found the right helpmate.

"That's why this is the perfect solution for Lily and me," she decided aloud. "Last month, when Ulysses suggested that I apply my employable skill to a better advantage, to help the family, I decided I'd do just that. I've given notice to Mr. Creighton that I'm taking the job as telegrapher in Julesberg, Colorado. He's already written me a letter of recommendation. Frankly, I'd rather not travel or live by myself. Letting Lily come with me is the perfect answer to everything. She'll be miles away from the order, and Ulysses won't have to concern himself with how to protect her."

Sayra reached into the pocket of her skirt and handed Bess the telegraph she'd received from a Truman Taylor, the Southwestern Division Supernumerary for Western Union. "I'll take care of her and send her to school. Surely they'll have formal schooling available. If not, I'll tutor her myself. Mr. Taylor asked me to leave on the first possible stage. There's trouble down the line, and he needs a replacement for the morning operator before he can investigate the problem. Lily will love the journey. You know how much she enjoys traveling, and she'll be more than a companion to me. She's such a joy."

Bess's eyes lit with hope. "You know, he might just agree to it."

"He must agree." Sayra refused to consider the alternative.

"Ulysses won't take kindly to being told what to do."

Impatience filled Sayra. "Bess, are you so afraid to challenge a wrong your husband is commiting that you're willing to put your own daughter in danger?"

"'Judge not lest ye be judged,'" Beth defended.

"You're right," Sayra apologized. Wrestling with her conscience for a moment, Sayra finally decided it wasn't wrong to use everything within her power to convince Bess that Lily must go to Julesberg. "Just look at her and tell me I'm wrong."

Both women glanced at sixteen-year-old Lily, playing cowboy and Indians with her four younger brothers while they attempted to ambush her at the corral. She held her arms out in invitation, and each of the dangerous-looking Indian counterparts flung down their makeshift lances and rushed into her loving arms, willingly surrendering to her hugs.

"Lord knows, Ulysses' good humor might return if he weren't having to worry about his cotton production and Lily's safety. Maybe if she went away for a while, he could forgive himself—" Bess whispered almost absentmindedly.

Compassion for her brother-in-law filled Sayra. "Lily's problems at birth weren't Ulysses' fault. The cord was wrapped around her neck, and Doc Given was nowhere to be found. Personally, I'm thankful he got back from town when he did, or she might have died instead."

A warm rush of love swept through Sayra as she examined Lily and her nephews from a distance and thanked God He had spared her niece. Lily brought such joy to all their lives, reminding them of simple pleasures by pointing them out in her uncomplicated, loving way.

To Sayra, the hope of raising her own children seemed an elusive dream. As elusive as finding the kind of man who would view a child in the same manner she did—a gift from God, no matter if others thought the child mentally inferior or less than whole. Perhaps this new turn of events was one of God's small blessings in disguise! She could safeguard Lily and, in return, Lily could become the child of her heart she might never physically have on her own.

"Do you think she'll ever be 'right'?" Bess asked wistfully, returning to take a seat in the rocker. A deep sadness filled her features. "Sometimes Ulysses wonders if he did the proper thing in saving her."

Horrified, her compassion for the man fled. Sayra grabbed the churn and began to work the cream furiously. "And you? Do you wonder the same?"

Wiping her hands on the apron tied around her linsey homespun, though they were still clean from the last time she'd wiped them, Bess grabbed Sayra's hands and halted their task. "Never. I've accepted God's will." Tears began to glisten in her eyes. "But I do wonder if she'll ever have any kind of normal life. Will she ever marry and find a measure of happiness of her own? Is there a special man out there to love someone like Lily?"

Despite her anger at Bess for not confronting the real issue being discussed—Bess and Ulysses were embarrassed by their daughter's slowness—Sayra's heart went out to her older sister, and she replied softly, "Ahh, Bess. We'll never know until she's away from here and allowed to live up to her potential, will we?"

Perhaps she was speaking for more than Lily now. *Maybe these words are meant for me, too,* Sayra decided. "Is there that kind of man for any of us? Only time will tell, and we can only trust in the Lord's Word that each of us has someone meant especially to love us. Just look at her, Sis," Sayra whispered, pleased that Lily had inherited her own cinnamon-colored hair and twilight-shaded eyes.

Many people complimented Sayra when her niece accompanied her, for most said they could have been mother and daughter. She never reminded anyone that she was only six years older than her niece, always feeling pleased at being thought Lily's parent. "She's such a blessing, Bess. Her soul is so gentle, and she only has kind words for everyone."

"Except to soldiers who deliberately shoot at a young boy's boots for the fun of watching him dance."

Concern clutched Sayra in its troublesome grip. "I doubt she would have ever told me about the incident if she could have gotten her father's attention long enough to protest to the authorities. But she was too scared to wait, Bess. She had to tell somebody about their vulgar insinuations. It was a good thing I came along when I did."

Though she said a silent, "Forgive me," to the Lord, Sayra could not hold back her admonishment. She must make her sister see reason, for Lily's sake. "Ulysses never seems to be around when Lily needs him." *And you won't act without his approval,* she added silently.

Bess began to pace the porch, making the planked boards bounce with each step. "He's just so busy nowadays. Those daily checks on the cotton inventory are taking all his time, and he's having to depend on his overseer to watch the fields. He comes home so tired, he eats supper then goes straight to bed. I rarely get to speak with him."

Sayra glanced at the workers in the adjacent cotton fields that once earned their parents a respectable living. Those same fields and work hands now provided the largest source of Ulysses Van Buren's income. A measure of forgiveness entered Sayra's thoughts for the first time that June morning. "Anyone with his responsibilities would have little time for anything. . .or anyone else," she admitted.

Anger clouded Bess's face as she stood. "Why can't you leave it alone?"

Sayra hadn't meant her last statement cruelly, but if Bess were going to remain defensive, then why not speak her own mind. . .now so they could really clear the air between them? Working the cream furiously, Sayra attempted to rid herself of the growing frustration that engulfed her. "Think of how aggravating it is to you not to have Ulysses' attention when you need it. How much more so for Lily, when often she can't think fast enough to say what needs to be said. I doubt I could endure the look of 'please hurry' in his eyes and the silent criticism that radiates from him when she fails to do or say something quickly enough for him. My heart aches for her. I just want to say, 'Slow down, Ulysses. Take time for her.'"

Raising the lid on the churn, Sayra checked the mixture's progress. "Remember how much it meant when Father left the fields and joined us for our sassafras tea parties? He never failed to make us feel as if his time with us was more precious than any he spent otherwise. How many times did he look into our playroom and simply say, 'Young misses, do you two have any idea how proud I am of you?'"

Bess stepped off the porch and turned her back to her children, misery etching her every feature. "He'll never let her go. He may not have time for her right now. But Ulysses couldn't endure her being away from his—"

"Protection?" Sayra laughed, the irony of it all knotting in her stomach. *Please do what's best for Lily*, she pleaded silently with her sister. A stronger wisdom than her own needed to be called upon, and she did so. *Thy will be done, Lord.*

"If you leave with her without his permission, Ulysses will never give you half of the inheritance."

Sayra felt Bess's change of heart as if were a soothing balm over sun-baked flesh. *Thank you, Lord.* She reached out and touched her sister gently, meeting Bess's gaze with purpose. "I'd give it up to take Lily away from here. . .at least for now, until the 'woman order' is revoked or Ulysses can take time to safeguard her. Give me *your* permission, Bess."

An unbidden tear brimmed in Bess's lashes and trickled down her cheek. She turned slowly, wiped it away with the back of one hand, and headed toward the corral. "Lily, come here, darling."

With cheeks flushed from twirling four-year-old Jimmy Don round and round, Lily ran toward her mother, eyes sparkling at Bess's approach. Sayra thought her niece never looked more childlike, and the weight of the responsibility she'd just taken on engulfed her. *I can do it,* she said silently, garnering her courage. *For Lily's sake and with Your help, God.*

"Mama, Jimmy's so much fun!" Lily exclaimed. "He made me laugh, and then he giggled so nice. Don't you just love the way he giggles?"

A momentous decision seemed imminent, urging Sayra to follow Bess's path. She watched her older sister's shoulders set, her spine straighten, and her chin lift a notch higher. Wanting to hear whatever conversation transpired between the two, Sayra moved closer to the corral.

Lily stood an inch taller than Bess. When she hugged her mother, Bess held on longer than usual. "Oohh, Mama, that kind of hurts. But hugs are 'specially nice, don't you think?"

Bess and Sayra shared a glance. Yes, Lily would always speak her mind, and nothing. . .particularly fear . . .should ever keep her from doing so.

"Yes, child." Bess let go abruptly. "Hugs are very nice, and sometimes they have to last for a long, long time."

Cupping a palm over her mouth to stifle a sob, Bess turned and stared out into the cotton fields while Lily returned to play with her brothers. "Take her."

"What about Ulysses?" Sayra took a step forward, but Bess put out a restraining hand that warned her to stay back.

"I'll deal with him."

"But—"

"There's money I've been saving in the sugar jar. It's not much, but it's all I can offer."

"I've got a little saved back myself," Sayra informed her, then placed her arm around her sister's shoulders. "You're doing the right thing, Sis. I prom—"

Bess moved away from Sayra's offered comfort. "Take her now. . .before I can't let her go."

two

Truman Taylor took out his watch fob and checked the time once again. His irritation grew along with the pile of telegrams stacking up on the desk in the Western Union Telegraph office of Julesburg, Colorado. After a while he clicked the fob closed and wondered if the next applicant would be on time or would keep an already busy man waiting.

He'd been through several interviews this morning and had a varied array of semiqualified applicants. Yet something didn't feel right about any of the choices, and he knew from past experience to follow his hunches.

Though he had received the telegram from S. A. Martin over two weeks ago, he supposed the telegrapher from Port Hudson had found a better position and decided not to head west, after all. For two days he kept the position open, hoping the lastest overland stage was merely delayed and the telegrapher would arrive shortly. Now it was going on the third day since Martin's planned appearance, and Tru simply couldn't wait any longer to fill the position.

It seemed the nation's brass pounders—as the telegraphers who transmitted Morse Code across the transcontinental line were called—were as in high demand in the South as they were here in the West. Northern loyalists who governed the southern territories wanted

16

to keep lines of communication well-tended in the event minor rebellions led to something more.

Truman thought it too good to be true when he first received the wire saying Martin wanted the position. Most brass pounders did not want to deal with the raiding renegades who cut the wire or the herds of buffalo that trampled the poles as fast as men could string them—or worse, used them as back scratchers for their hairy hides. All that seemed minor compared to suffering the general lack of supplies that were, instead, sold to southern markets for hiked prices and fast profit.

Having a skilled telegrapher to man the Julesburg station seemed as likely as the next applicant being a better prospect than those he'd already interviewed. Still, somewhere out there in the streets of the muddy Colorado town, there had to be a good hand at the keys. One who wouldn't mind long hours and would appreciate fair pay when the bankroll didn't get ambushed. One who prided himself on having a good ear for the code and could get along with some of the more temperamental receivers who worked either side of the line.

A miracle is what I need, Truman decided.

The sound of shoes being wiped on the planked sidewalk outside revealed the arrival of the next applicant.

At least he's thoughtful, Truman acknowledged with approval. *Maybe he'll be tidy, too.* A glance at the messy desk and scattered telegrams urged a loud, "Hurrumphh!" from Truman. *This place could use some order.*

"Now you wait outside here, Lily, and I'll see if it's all right to invite you in. Don't go anywhere without me—okay?"

The voice was definitely feminine, causing Truman to squint toward the oilcloth window covers. The applicant must be late. Another glance at his watch before depositing it in the pocket of his buckskin trousers deepened Tru's disapproval. Time was always of the essence in this business, and the applicant would soon learn his lack of concern for it would prove the reason he didn't get the job. . .if the man ever showed up.

The owner of flat, Mary Jane slippers, a butternut serge travel suit, and matching bonnet stepped into the telegraph shack.

"May I help you, miss?" Truman inquired, standing abruptly and setting some of the telegrams awry.

"Mr. Truman Taylor?"

"Yes," Truman replied, frankly admiring the blue of her eyes, which reminded him of a lake he'd once seen in the Ozarks. Sun-kissed mahogany curls framed her face, and he found himself attracted to one of the finest-looking women he'd ever had the privilege of meeting.

"My name is Sayra Martin, and I'm here in answer to your telegram. I had a bit of difficulty leaving Port Hudson as soon as I expected and—"

"Sayra Martin? S. A. Martin?" While trying to locate her recent telegram amidst the clutter, he scattered more papers in front of the desk.

She bent and gathered them, holding them out to Truman. "You must have expected a man."

When he took her offering, their fingers touched. Though she wore kid gloves, he felt as if they'd exchanged more than papers. "I did," he admitted. "Frankly, I'm not prepared for a woman. As you can see, I didn't clean up the office. . . I mean, most of the telegraphers we hire tend to sleep here in the shack and call it home."

He offered a smile of apology and waved at the cot that stood in one corner. An oil lamp and chair had been provided for reading. A potbellied stove and instruments necessary to transfer the messages cross country took up the largest amount of space. "It's not much to look at, but it's serviceable."

"I'm sure it will be just fine, Mr. Taylor," Sayra assured him. No need for him to think she expected any more than he would have given a male counterpart. "Especially with a bit of straightening."

"Please have a seat, Miss Martin," Truman offered, seeing the stacks of paper and clutter as she must view them. Someone named Lily waited outside, if he remembered correctly. Perhaps he should remind her. "It is Miss, isn't it? Did you bring a friend with you?"

She motioned toward the door. "Yes to both questions. May my niece come in as well? I dislike leaving her outside alone in an unfamiliar place. She'll be no bother, I assure you."

"That's a good idea. Julesburg is relatively safe, but because we connect with a couple of the overland trails, we sometimes get some hard characters in town." With every passing moment, he wondered how he could give a woman this job. The long hours would be too taxing on her. And the receivers weren't exactly easy with the language that came across the wire. No, this just wasn't going to work.

"May I introduce my niece, Mr. Truman? This is Lily Van Buren, of the Port Hudson Van Burens." Sayra exchanged introductions for Lily and motioned her niece to sit in the chair next to the one she had taken in front of his desk. Laying her purse in her lap, Lily folded her hands and rested them in the middle of her reticule.

Niece? The girl could have been the woman's daughter, they looked so much alike. Both had porcelain complexions that gave their high cheekbones a dusky-rose color. But their eyes captured and held his attention. Like the blue-violet hues that blanketed the jagged peaks of the Rockies just after sundown, their eyes asked him to move mountains. To take a chance on them, despite the fact that they were women. Trusting eyes that needed something more than he was certain he could give.

"You're real handsome, Mr. Taylor," Lily complimented, looking at her aunt for agreement. "His hair looks like coal. Shiny black coal. And his eyes are greener than mountain mint. He's awfully handsome, isn't he, Sayra?"

Heat traveled up Truman's neck and erupted across his own cheeks, convincing him that he'd blushed for the first time in his twenty-eight years. "Thank y-you, Miss Van Buren. Rarely has anyone paid me such a compliment."

"Well they should." Lily nudged Sayra. "In the Bible it says to 'do unto others as you would have them do unto you.' Sayra calls me pretty, and that's the way she makes me feel when she says it. I wouldn't tell you you're handsome if I didn't really mean it, would I, Sayra?"

Glad Lily had given her a way out of answering her opinion about his attractiveness, Sayra kindly responded, "No, Lily, you wouldn't speak an untruth." As she handed her possible employer her credentials, she offered to put him at ease. "I hope we haven't made you feel uncomfortable, Mr. Taylor. It's just that Lily says what she feels, and I, for one, think it's refreshing."

"Please, the both of you must call me Tru or Truman, in the least. I like to get to know my telegraphers on a more personal basis."

"Then I have the job?"

He flipped through the pages she handed him. The list of credentials was neat and clean. A letter of recommendation from the Port Hudson division of Western Union seemed impressive, to say the least. He was familiar with the supernumerary there, and its management seldom, if ever, went to the trouble to offer such high recommendation. If she were half as good as her references indicated, he had just hired the next telegrapher for Julesburg, no matter what her gender.

"It says you lived in Port Hudson most of your life, Miss Martin. May I call you Sayra?" At her nod of acquiesence, he continued, "What made you choose to leave your home? I don't mean to pry, but I would like to know if there's any chance of you changing your mind and returning soon. I'm looking for a long-term employee I can trust to help Benjamin keep this end of the line going."

He nodded toward a map pinned to the wall. An X marked the stations along the transcontinental route, strung together by the California Telegraph Company from the west and the Western Union from the east. "As I mentioned before, there are various areas along the line. Headquarters is up near South Pass, but we're stringing line in some of the smaller settlements just west of Denver. I'm needed up near Georgetown at the moment. Can you make Julesburg your home?"

"You aren't prying, Mr. Taylor. And who is Benjamin?"

"Truman, please."

Something about his voice made her want to test his name upon her lips. "Truman," she acknowledged.

"Ben is the night telegrapher. You'll work from seven 'til seven, and he'll take the other twelve-hour shift. He was due back on the same stage you two came in on."

Sayra nodded. "The man with smiling eyes?"

"Yes, that's Ben. Smiles so much, his eyes kind of fade into his lashes."

"I remember him saying he'd best get some sleep because it would be the last he'd get once Tru knew he was back. I didn't realize he was talking about you."

"Well, enough about Ben. What about you, Sayra?"

Hesitation filled her. How much did one tell a stranger she hoped to befriend? "Lily and I moved from Port Hudson so we could begin a life of our own alone and in a new place. We won't be going back. . .unless our money won't hold out until you pay me, Truman."

His name sounded different coming from her soft Southern drawl. Musical. . .gentle. . .descriptions not often associated with him. More than that, it sounded right as if it belonged there. "You don't worry about that. I'll advance you two months' wages, and you can pay me back a bit of it at a time over the next year. We never know when a payroll's going to be ambushed, so you'd best take the offer while we've got it in the bank to advance you."

Her chin lifted a notch higher. "Only if you'll take out one-twelfth of what I owe you every month before you give me my wages."

The woman had a streak of pride in her, that was for certain. The fact that she accepted the money was all he needed to know. She meant to plant roots here, and that's what counted at the moment.

A message ticked out over the wire. *Click, click, clickety-click.* Tru frowned, mentally deciphering the series of dots and dashes that said the trouble at the next station couldn't wait.

"Who's Jubilee?" Sayra asked, stepping forward and bending one ear toward the keys. "Is there a doctor to fix his leg?"

Good, Tru thought. *If she can read Molly's clumsy fist on the keys, then she's worth giving this chance.*

"Jubilee's up at Badger Springs. He's broken his leg climbing the pole to repair a wire that blew down in last night's windstorm. Molly is Jube's wife and, bless her heart, has learned enough code to at least get this to us. Excuse me for a minute, and I'll see if she can man the shack 'til I can get there." Tru reached for the wire and began tapping the key, transmitting his question.

Mst go. C Doc. Now! The clicks ended as abruptly as her answer.

"She won't stay!" Tru announced in frustration.

Sayra watched her new boss brush his hands through the dark hair that waved at his temples and curled to the collar of his buckskin shirt. "She wants to be with her husband," she reminded gently, trying to console the worry narrowing Truman's emerald eyes.

"I know," he sighed heavily, "but I can't leave the wire unattended, and it's unfair to ask Ben to handle both shifts alone."

Sayra stood and grabbed the slouch hat that hung on a peg beside the door, extending it to him. "Then go," she insisted. "I'll take care of this end. That's what you asked me to come here to do anyway. Why not let me do my job?"

His gaze searched her face, and he realized she'd already lived up to her credentials. "Guess there's no time like now for jumping in, is there?"

"I'll be fine." She shooed him toward the door.

"But I haven't showed you where anything is or how to do things our way," he protested. Despite his words, his long legs had already propelled him out onto the planked sidewalk and toward the sorrel saddled in front of the shack.

Sayra watched him, admiring the fluid agility and muscular physique that hinted that he spent many of his days outdoors rather than poised in front of the telegraph keys. "I know how I do things, and that'll have to do until Ben gets here," she replied. "As for where things are, I'll just do the best I can in finding them."

Truman reined the horse half-quarter. "Remind me to thank you when I have more time, all right? And before I forget, go over to the bank and tell Hiram to advance you the money we spoke of. He knows the standard wages and can draw up an agreement, if you like. Personally, I only need your word."

"You have it, Mr. Taylor." Sayra shielded her eyes from the glaring sun as she stared up at him. "And thanks for the loan."

"It's you who are doing me the favor, Sayra." A smile stretched across his lips, revealing a blaze of white, well-tended teeth. "And hopefully by the time I get back, you'll feel a little easier calling me Tru."

His departure left her feeling both disappointed and elated. Disappointment filled her when she realized his leaving would keep them from getting to know each other better. Truman Taylor seemed a congenial, if busy, man. But more than his friendliness, she found herself attracted to her boss—a fact that she would keep uppermost in mind so it wouldn't interfere with her duties. But nothing said they couldn't become friends. When Truman returned, she and Lily would invite him over for supper.

Hope filled her with elation. Meeting a new friend and finding the job still available to her made Sayra feel that her life was headed down a better path. It was the first time in a long while she'd experienced that feeling.

three

The sound of the telegraph instrument ticking off a message captured Sayra's attention, and she immediately set to work recording the message. While she jotted down the incoming telegram, she asked, "Lily, sweet, would you mind getting a cloth out of my paisley carpetbag and start dusting? I'll take care of this as soon as possible; then we'll both do some straightening before this Benjamin fellow gets here this evening."

"Sure, Aunt Sayra. It'll be fun." Lily opened the door to the shack and started to drag in the heavy trunk they'd left outside on the sidewalk.

"Wait a minute," Sayra scribbled as fast as she could, "and I'll help you with that one. I don't want you to strain yourself. Get the smaller one while I finish this—"

A man in an army-issued uniform appeared at the doorway. He tipped his hat and said, "I'd love to help the young miss, if I may."

"Well certainly, but I wouldn't want to put you to any trouble."

"No trouble at all, ma'am." He gently took the trunk from Lily's grasp and began to scoot it himself. "It's a pure pleasure, in fact."

"Excuse me a moment," Sayra apologized while trying to concentrate on sending a confirmation to the Kansas operator. But concentration proved difficult. After all, trouble with soldiers was the reason they had left Port Hudson. *Msg received,* she tapped. *Wll snd when Badger Springs is properly manned again.*

Thank U, the message ticked back.

Sayra moved from behind the desk and bent to help the soldier complete the task he'd so readily accepted. It was wrong to sit in judgment of this soldier simply because he wore the same uniform as those back home. "My niece and I really appreciate this, sir."

He rose and brushed a sleeve across his brow, bumping his hat up to reveal sandy-colored hair. The soldier gave Lily an appreciative glance. "If you'll pardon my asking, I was wondering if you ladies are new in town? I know I haven't seen you before, or I would have shown you both a real Julesberg welcome. Are you visiting, or do you plan on adding your beauty to our township for a goodly time?"

Lily giggled as she carried in the carpetbag Sayra had requested. "I think he likes us, Aunt Sayra, but he sure says it in a funny way."

"Lily!" Sayra forced down her own chuckle as her face heated with a flush. "He's just glad to see new faces."

The soldier smiled broadly, his brown eyes darkening to warm amber. "Your niece is delightfully correct, Miss—?" He paused for an appropriate introduction.

Sayra told him their names and asked his own.

"Major Parker Quinton," he half-bowed and lifted Lily's gloved hand to his lips, pressing a kiss along her fingertips that did not quite make contact with the glove. "Please say you're staying."

"My aunt is the new telegrapher," Lily boasted, pulling her hand away. She rocked back and forth on the balls of her feet, setting the flounce of her red skirt into a swishing motion. " 'Course, she didn't make this mess. We just arrived, and it was cluttered before we got here. Mr. Taylor wants us to clean it up."

Rushing to her employer's defense, Sayra started to pick up the telegram from Molly, then remembered that Truman had not written the message down. "He had to go to the next station. It seems a Mr. Jubilee broke his leg."

Parker's forehead furrowed, making his dust-colored brows point like daggers over his eyes. "And left you here alone on your first day? I must speak with the man about his manners."

Sayra hid a smile behind a gloved hand and pretended to sneeze to cover her mirth. As far as she was concerned Mr. Jubilee's broken leg took precedence over any lack of good manners. "I'm sure he regrets leaving a newcomer in charge in his absence. And someone by the name of Benjamin is to take over for me at seven. So we're not completely without aid."

Major Quinton looked around at the clutter. "You could use some help cleaning the place. May I lend a hand?"

A small prayer of thanks whispered through Sayra's thoughts. Though she was prepared to complete the necessary cleaning herself, both she and Lily were tired from the rattle and sway of the stage. Every bone in her body felt as if it had been jarred from its joint. A lending hand seemed an awfully nice surprise. "I must admit, I wondered how Lily and I were going to move the desk around so I could sweep well. And it all needs better positioning to give us more room."

"Well, then let me be of assistance." He headed toward the entryway where a broom stood in the corner.

To Sayra's amazement, he continued walking and announced over his shoulder, "I'll be back."

Lily stared at him in confusion. "Do you think maybe Major Quinton forgot he said he would help, Aunt Sayra?"

Sayra laughed. "No, sweet. I believe he's going to do what officers do best. . .get someone else to help us in his stead."

Less than fifteen minutes later, a work party of four soldiers arrived with mops, buckets, and rolled-up sleeves. Despite her and Lily's protests that all they needed was for the men to lift furniture, each private assigned himself to one fourth of the shack and began scrubbing from floor to ceiling. Each also seemed a most congenial man.

Sayra and Lily insisted upon filing and separating the paperwork atop Truman's desk. Upon her request, the workers moved the desk to one side of the room, the cot to the other, and allowed all the necessary tools to be arranged consecutively from left to right so the process would flow easily. Dust no longer layered the backs of chairs or the tops of shelves. Everything gleamed, and the air smelled fresh with pinion oil. Sayra could actually see out the newly brushed oilcloth windows.

"How can I ever thank you?" Sayra asked, gratitude for their Christian charity making her wish she and Lily had already found lodgings and could invite them to supper.

"It was our pleasure, Miss Martin," Major Quinton

replied, ordering the others to prepare to leave. "Anything the army can do to make your stay here more permanent, please let us know."

She thanked each one of them as they left, promising a home-cooked meal once she and Lily were settled.

"Perhaps you'll agree to ride with me after church Sunday." Major Quinton directed his question to Sayra, but his gaze never left Lily's figure as she returned the duster and other personal cleaning tools into the trunk.

A feeling of unease swept through Sayra, and she stepped between the major and her niece. *How utterly foolish,* she reprimanded silently, warning herself that she could not judge every soldier by those who had been cruel to Lily. The man had done nothing out of the ordinary to make her feel any misgiving; neither was his look anything but of deep interest.

I'm just being overprotective, Sayra decided. "We'd love to accept your company, Major. Shall we sit together at church as well?"

The look in the soldier's eyes seem to take on a glint. "I won't be able to attend services, Miss Martin. But I will have a buggy at your and your lovely niece's disposal as soon as they are finished."

Politeness kept her from asking whether his duties would keep him from attending or whether he seldom frequented the Lord's house. "We'll bring a picnic basket."

"Aunt Sayra, won't you have to work? Mr. Taylor didn't say anything about a day of rest," Lily reminded.

Sayra smiled apologetically. "Where may I send you a message? I'll ask Mr. Benjamin if I'm to have a day off. I meant to request that I have at least enough time off on Sunday to attend church services. If I'm scheduled to work, perhaps he'll change shifts with me, or at least stay until after services. We might have to decline the buggy ride and picnic, if that's the case."

"You can reach me at the post, but why not let me talk to Ben when he comes in?" Major Quinton drew himself up to offer a more commanding appearance, setting his jaw rigidly, his shoulders and chest filling out the blue uniform to its seams.

With a shake of her head, Sayra refused his help. "I'll talk to Mr. Benjamin myself. We're co-workers now, and I'd rather not make him feel I'm attempting to get out of work and enlisting help to do so, even before I officially meet the man. I'm sure the Lord will understand if I visit His house later in the evening, if duty requires. Surely you understand the value of duty, Major Quinton."

"Indeed, I do, Miss Martin. I will await your message and bid you a good evening." The officer bowed low.

"The same to you, Major Quinton."

He strolled over to Lily and reached for her hand, lifting it to his lips. "'Til another day, Miss Van Buren, of which I hope there will be many."

Sayra noted his mouth did not halt inches from Lily's hand, but pressed lips to flesh.

Lily pulled back her hand and giggled. "I thought you were going to bite me like my brother, Jimmy Don, does. But that kind of felt nice. Sort of tingly."

A broad smile flashed across Major Quinton's face, his eyes sparkling with the mirth that soon followed.

"Had I known it would bring such a delightful sound into my life, I would have done this much sooner. But unfortunately, I must leave you now." With a half-bow, he bade them good evening.

Why his frank interest and approval of Lily bothered Sayra caused her to question her feelings for a long time after his leaving. Perhaps she thought Major Quinton a bit too old for her niece. Yet, he couldn't have been more than six or seven years older, barely older than Sayra. That didn't seem such a broad age difference. Maybe it was that he too readily saw her niece's beauty and delighted in her innocence. But if that were true, she'd be equally guilty of the same innameable crime of which she was accusing the major.

The wire began to tick a new message, and Sayra immediately stored the worry for later. As she deciphered the incoming news, she decided the real answer lay within herself. She'd told Bess she wanted to take Lily where her niece could have an adult life. Now, when the first man showed interest, she instantly became the she-bear watching over her cub.

Faith must begin somewhere, if they were to get on with their lives. She must believe that Lily was ready for the world Sayra hoped to give her and that Major Parker Quinton was an honorable man who did not play lightly with a young woman's trust and affection.

I need to practice what I preach, Sayra thought with conviction as she finished transcribing the telegram. *Lily can decide whether or not she's ready to be courted. But nothing says I can't go along to chaperone.*

"Hey, was that Major Quinton I saw leaving here?"

asked the balding man as he stepped into the telegraph shack and stopped dead still in his stride. "Jehosophat! I haven't seen this place this clean in *years!*"

Sayra stood and offered her hand to the smiling-eyed man who had rode in the stage with them for a good part of the journey. "You must be Mr. Benjamin." She made the introductions and admitted, "We can't take all the credit for the cleaning. Major Quinton had a detail team help in the scrubbing."

"That's a first!" Benjamin slapped his hat on his thigh, sending dust from its brim. "Oops. Sorry, ma'am."

Her own misgivings suddenly resurfaced. "You don't sound as if you have a high opinion of the major, Mr. Benjamin."

"Ben," he insisted. "Ben Balou but just plain Ben. No, I don't cotton to Major Quinton. Some say he'd as soon as swindle ya as look at ya. But he hasn't ever done me any wrong, so I figure judge not lest ye be judged. Right, ma'am?"

Her throat constricted and dried, making it difficult to swallow. Though she had worried every day since taking Lily from her parents that she might have judged Ulysses unfairly and should have given him time to deal with the situation in his own way, everything within Sayra warned her to proceed with caution in her dealings with Major Quinton. "You're right of course, sir, but I've also been taught to shake the dust from my feet and walk away if he shows himself to be the kind of man Lily and I should not be acquainted with."

"Don't you be worrying about that," Ben assured her.

"Major Quinton will toe the mark as long as Truman Taylor's around. Since it was Tru who brought you out here for a job, he'll personally consider it his duty to see you are treated kindly."

"My niece and I have managed quite nicely on our own during our overland trip, and I don't foresee a change in those capabilities." Offering such help would be fine and good, Sayra thought, but Truman Taylor was already not "around" to troubleshoot for them. And if she remembered the distance correctly, Badger Springs was a long way to ride in order to head off any trouble Major Quinton might pose.

four

Julesberg was abustle with wagons and teamsters stopping to replenish supplies before heading north to the Boseman Trail, northwest into the Oregon Trail, west along the Kearney Trail, or south toward the Sante Fe and Butterfield overland routes.

Every size, shape, religion, color, and creed of mankind filled the streets and businesses that formed the Colorado settlement. Telegraph business was good, for most paid a visit to send their regards to loved ones back East or to inform someone in the West of their impending arrival. Major Quinton had been into the office at least three times in less than twenty-four hours—a testament that he was either extremely dedicated to sending the fort's correspondence or enamored of Lily.

Sayra glanced up from the keys and offered the major a smile as he strolled into the shack and took off his hat. "Back so soon, Major Quinton?"

His face reddened as he stepped aside to let her most recent customer pass through the doorway. "I'm not here to send a telegram, this time, Miss Martin. I wondered if you and Miss Van Buren would do me the honor of dining with me?"

Glancing at the ormalu clock that sat on one edge of the desk, Sayra realized the time. Her shoulders and neck ached from having poised over the keys for nearly twelve hours, tapping out countless messages. Her shift was almost over, and Lily would arrive any moment to join her for dinner.

She felt disappointed, because she had hoped to hear from Truman before leaving for the day. "Lily should be here in a few minutes," Sayra informed the major. "I let her sleep in and relax. It had been such a long stage ride and literally days since we've had a decent place to sleep."

"You were fortunate Mrs. Kou had that cancellation at the boarding house."

Images of the saffron-colored comforter and curtains gracing the four-poster bed and windows brought a smile to Sayra's lips. The immaculate, fresh-smelling room the Greek landlady offered them last night, after Sayra's shift, seemed like an oasis from heaven. Weeks of traveling along rutted, sandy roads made Sayra fear she and Lily would never be rid of all the grit in their lashes. Her eyes had only stopped watering a few hours ago, and she'd noticed she hadn't sneezed in a while. Yes, Mrs. Koumalapalous—Mrs. Kou, as the Julesberg inhabitants chose to call her—was a godsend.

"Aunt Sayra? Are you almost ready to go?" Lily flounced in, looking very much like a model out of Godey's Lady's Book. Dressed in a violet teagown that complimented her youthful figure and the dusky rose of her cheeks, Lily seemed unaware of the attention she drew from the men who stopped along the sidewalk to admire and stare after her.

"Good evening, Miss Van Buren." Major Quinton bowed deeply, approval shining in the depths of his brown eyes. His silent appraisal began at the tip of her lavender Morroco slippers and ended at the plume rising jauntily at one angle from the crown of her hat. "May I say you look extremely lovely tonight."

Lily twirled around, first one way, then the next, tossing a cinnamon-colored ringlet behind her shoulder. "Don't I though? But it's because of the gown. Mrs. Koumalapalous gave it to me. A whole trunk of them! And she dressed my hair, too."

A feeling of gratitude warmed Sayra's heart. She'd have to thank Mrs. Kou personally for her kindness. Lily was not destitute of clothing by any means, but she owned nothing this exquisitely made. The woman had no way of knowing that the luxury of having her hair curled by someone else was a particular thrill to Lily.

Lily sat down on the chair beside Sayra and smoothed out the folds in the fabric. She rested one elbow on the desk and leaned closer, as if sharing a secret. "This belonged to her daughter, you know. Melina. Isn't that the most beautiful name you ever heard? Melina Koumalapalous. Kinda like licking a sucker a whole bunch of times. Melina Koumalapalous. Say it. See what I mean? Kind of tastes sweet, just saying it."

Lily was right, Sayra decided, repeating the name.

"But you see," Lily's voice lowered into a conspiratorial whisper, "Melina ran off with a trapper, and Mrs. Koumalapalous didn't know why she left or where they went to." Puzzlement creased her brow. "Why would anyone run away from her parents?"

A twinge of guilt filled Sayra, and she discovered she couldn't look Lily in the eye. Hadn't she done that very thing? Made Lily run away from her father's lack of action without facing the real issue? Grabbing a stack of telegrams, Sayra busied her hands with alphabetizing them by the sender's last name. Major Quinton seemed aware of her unease, and she didn't want him asking questions that were none of his business. An answer to Lily's question would be necessary to waylay his curiosity.

She placed the telegrams in a neat pile and gently reached for her niece's hand. Lily willingly gave her both to be cupped into Sayra's palms. "You see, Blossom," Sayra began, using the nickname she'd chosen years ago for the fragile beauty who owned a piece of her heart, "sometimes people run because they think it's the best thing to do at the moment. It often takes time and a little distance to be able to think clearly and determine if they made a wise decision. I'm sure when Melina's ready, she'll come back and face whatever made her leave."

Major Quinton seemed to lean closer as well, making Sayra all too aware he sensed there was something more to the explanation she offered Lily. She resisted the impulse to ask him if he knew what such curiosity supposedly did to cats.

The bell atop the office door jingled, announcing Benjamin's arrival. Sayra let go of her niece's hands and offered a welcome to her replacement. "Ready for work?" she asked, grateful for his timely interruption. "I'm afraid I still haven't heard from Mr. Taylor."

"Ahh, don't worry about Tru." Benjamin walked in and hung his slouch hat on a hook behind the door. Rubbing his bald head, as if there were mussed hair to straighten, he looked up and realized everyone probably thought the action was useless. "He's more than likely got the line up and running by now. My guess is he's trying to catch up with what has to get done. Tru'll contact us soon as he feels he caught up enough to let us know everything's okay." Ben nodded briefly at the major. "Evening, Quinton."

"Balou." The soldier nodded in return, their disrespect for one another apparent in the fact they acknowledged each other only by their last names.

Ben picked up the neat pile of telegrams and scanned them. "Truman will be pleased. Looks like you've got a real handle on things around here."

Sayra rose from behind the desk to allow him to take his position. "I'm grateful for all those instructions you gave before you left this morning. It made things go a lot easier. Mr. Taylor's filing system is unique, to say the least."

A chuckle made the bald man's cheeks dimple. "You can say that again. He don't follow any alphabet I know. Says they're listed in order of priority: had to do, finally did, and will get around to doing."

The two sisters joined him in laughter.

When Major Quinton cleared his throat, Sayra was reminded she had never given the man a genuine answer to his request. She directed her words to Lily, "Would you like to have supper with Major Quinton? He's been kind enough to ask."

Lily's eyes sparkled as she offered him her rapt attention. "Will you finish telling me all about the time you were Stonewall Jackson's second in a duel? This morning at breakfast, you were interrup—"

"You two had breakfast together this morning?"

Surprise filled Sayra as her brows arched in question.

"He came to visit Mrs. Koumalapalous, and she invited him to stay," Lily informed. "I got to sit by him and listen to his wonderful story."

He half-bowed. "I'm glad to know my exploits are of interest to you."

Sayra shared a glance with Benjamin. When his eyes focused heavenward, the knot of tension that had instantly risen in her throat, suddenly subsided into a giggle. Both suspected the evening would be spent listening to the soldier's tales of daring-do. Major Quinton obviously had two categories of action, "does" and "wants to do."

"Excuse me," she cleared her throat and coughed. *There you go again,* she reprimanded herself, embarrassed that she had to hide her chuckle. *Judging again. The man's been nothing but nice to you and Lily.* Feeling ashamed of herself, Sayra tried to offer her sincerest smile. "I'm sure we'll *both* be interested, Major Quinton. A soldier of your rank must have numerous tales. . .er. . .experiences to share with those of us who depend on you."

Quinton placed his hat on his head and offered an arm to each of the ladies. "A good deal many more than a man has a right to acknowledge, Miss Martin."

"Sayra, please," she insisted, trying to put aside her initial misgivings about the man. He was only attempting to be neighborly, and she should do the same.

"Only if I may call your lovely niece Lily, as well. As I would want her to call me Parker. Both of you, of course."

Lily nodded, setting her curls and bonnet to bobbing.

"It's all right with us, Parker. Isn't it, Aunt Sayra?"

"Certainly." Though she agreed, Sayra could not shed an indiscernible forboding that she should tread carefully around Parker Quinton—all was not as it should be with the man. Yet she could not condemn his actions so far. Perhaps she was just too ready to suspect any man's actions toward her niece.

"We'd best be on our way or the Congress will be filled to capacity," Major Quinton warned. "Sourdough Jones said he'd save a table for me 'til a quarter after, but if I arrived later than that he couldn't make any promises."

"Then by all means," Sayra linked her arm through his and waited until Lily did the same, "lead the way."

Click. Click. Clickety-click. A message began to tick out over the wire. Sayra stopped still and listened to the dots and dashes. "Wait a minute. It's Truman," she insisted, unlinking her arm. Reading the expression of hurry that darted across the soldier's face, she assured him it wouldn't take long.

Benjamin jotted down the words. "Said the line's up, but not really going yet. Jubilee's seen the doc and has to stay in bed at least a week." The night telegrapher glanced up, embarrassed. "Sorry, Miss Martin. I'm used to curious people being in the office and not knowing how to make it all out. I usually just tell them what's being said unless I know it's meant for only certain ears. Old habit."

She shrugged off his explanation. "No need to apologize. I'd probably do the same thing." She paused to listen. "What's that about Jubilee's wife?"

Benjamin started writing again, his bald head bent

over the paper as he concentrated on the incoming message.

"I hate to complain, Sayra," Major Quinton interrupted, "but we're going to lose the table if we don't go."

Torn between chaperoning Lily and hearing the transmission that asked her to remain if she had not already left, Sayra tossed the alternatives around in her head. The restaurant was only across the street. Easy access if Lily needed her. Sayra's decision was made.

"You two go on and order me whatever both of you are having," she finally conceded. "I'll be there as soon as I can."

Major Quinton flashed Lily a broad, even-toothed grin. His eyes darkened to warm chocolate as he pressed his hand over the smaller one linked through his. "I'm sure Sweet Lily and I can find something to amuse ourselves with until your return. Please don't hurry on our account."

"I wouldn't think of leaving you two alo—" Sayra almost embarrassed herself. She had to think fast. "alone to explain to Mr. Sourdough why I didn't show up to eat what I had ordered. I hear he's adamant you eat everything you order. . .because of supplies being so difficult to come by and all."

Benjamin shook his head. She shot him a warning glance, then quickly turned her attention back to Lily and her escort. "I'll be right along. I'm sure, whatever Mr. Taylor needs, it won't take but a moment."

"Don't worry if it does." Parker headed for the door. "We can always bring you a plate."

The night telegrapher waited until the couple left

before handing Sayra the rest of the message. "Wrong . . .he's asked you to stand by tonight while I ride in to Badger Springs and help him. Looks like you and Sourdough's going to have a difference of opinion."

She watched the couple's progress across the street, noting how Parker Quinton steered her niece away from a mule skinner's team that passed them. His hand had unlinked and now wrapped itself around Lily's waist— a protective action but unnecessary. The team was yards away from posing a threat.

"I can handle an angry cook," Sayra announced, "it's the woman-hungry major who's my biggest concern at the moment."

five

The evening progressed with scattered messages from Truman. Flames rose above the lantern's wick, flickering as wind billowed the oilcloth windows of the telegraph office. Chills raced over Sayra's cheeks and neck, ending in an icy pool at the base of her spine.

She grabbed a poker and stoked the coals inside the Franklin stove, warding off a nip in the air that blanketed Julesberg with night mists. Ignoring an impulse to fetch the shawl Lily had brought over from their room, along with her valise, Sayra decided a little bit of cold would keep her alert and less ready to indulge in the drowsiness that hooded her eyes the past hour. Thank goodness, her worry over Major Quinton had been needless. He'd escorted Lily back to the office after their meal and kindly accompanied Lily both to and from the boarding house to bring Sayra the valise.

After pouring herself a cup of coffee, Sayra sipped it and welcomed the flood of heat down her throat. The telegraph machine had remained quiet for more than thirty minutes; no incoming or outgoing messages. After the busy two days since her arrival, Sayra was grateful for the respite. She searched the valise and found her hairbrush. Brushing her hair always revived her, making her feel as if she could work longer, if required. Right now anything would help stave off the exhaustion settling in her bones. How does Truman

Taylor manage to work round-the-clock for days? she wondered.

Seated across from the telegraph keys, Sayra worked her brush through thick, cinnamon-colored curls until they shone like sunlight glinting off mahogany. Then she wove them into a single, thick braid. When the keys began to click with a message from Truman, embarrassment filled her as if he'd walked into the room and caught her in the middle of dressing.

"Yes. Stop. Still here. Stop," she answered aloud as she tapped, glad he couldn't see the blush that heated her cheeks. "Intended receiver of this message? Stop."

No one. Stop. Just wanted to talk. Stop. All quiet here. Stop. Thought we could keep each other alert. Stop.

While his message ticked out over the wire, she no longer heard the stops. . .as if they were having a normal conversation. Sayra frowned, imagining how tired he must be. "When will Ben reach you?" she asked. "He left less than an hour after your request."

Several hours, if there's no trouble. So, we've got some time to spare. Want to play "Taps"?

"What's that?"

A game some of us play when there's nothing going on and we need to prop our eyes open. One of us starts talking until we get tired, then the other takes over until our fingers are too tired for us to tap. If you happen to get a customer, simply tap out. We can pick up where we left off once business slows again. Sound interesting?

Interesting? Sayra's fingers paused before answering. She wanted to know more about her employer and become friends with him but wasn't certain how much she should tell him about her and Lily. "What sort of things would we discuss?"

Anything. Nothing, in particular. For instance. . .your hesitation just now tells me you're not the talkative sort. Most women I've had the questionable pleasure of meeting chatter in seasons instead of nights. Think you can keep up the game until dawn?

When she realized he was challenging her, Sayra flexed her fingers, straightened her back, and accepted the dare. "You start."

Clever move. All right then, I'm sitting here in the telegrapher's tent, staring out the front flap at the night stars. It puts me in a—

"A tent?" The wire hummed with her surprise. "Badger Springs doesn't have a wooden shack as command post?"

Every telegraph station she'd ever worked for had provided the best working conditions. Her respect grew for those of her profession who chose to string the wire west. What other adverse conditions did they suffer?

We don't have one yet. Like the pioneer he was, Truman's answer held no blame toward the Western Union. *But that's fine until fall sets in. Maybe we can do something about it now that you're here, and Ben can give me a hand occasionally. But enough about business. . . I guess I could start by telling you what you'd want to know about your employer.*

Sayra listened intently, discovering that he'd grown up in Texas, been a Pony Express rider at fifteen, a scout for the army at seventeen, and worked for the Western Union ever since. In turn, she told him that she'd lived in St. Louis as a child and moved to Port

Hudson when her grandfather passed away and her father inherited the plantation.

When Truman asked how she became a telegrapher, she told of how Edward Creighton visited Port Hudson and made quite a stir among the townpeople when he said women were better on the line than men, because they were quicker with their hands. She'd been chosen out of the audience to prove his claim. Creighton thought her such a natural talent, and since she was unmarried and without usual family obligations, he'd insisted she learn the code and man the Port Hudson station when the regulars needed time off with their families. It became a blessing, for the position allowed her an income separate from the one resulting from the cotton fields. What she didn't tell Truman was that she was fiercely independent and had only taken from Ulysses what she felt was rightfully her share. Otherwise, she had paid her own way.

Minutes developed into hours, and suddenly dawn appeared, filtering rays through the oilcloth windows. "This is a wonderful game," Sayra complimented as warmth emanated from the long-used keys. "Almost as wonderful as staring up at the sunrise and realizing it's a new day and you can start all over again."

You do that, too?

"That's usually when I plan." Memories of all the mornings she'd spent since leaving Port Hudson flooded her thoughts and reminded Sayra of the hopes that had risen in her heart each of those dawns. Hope that she was doing the right thing. That she hadn't been unfair to Bess and Ulysses in her effort to protect Lily.

"Lots of people I know stare at the night sky and

reflect on past mistakes and try to find a way to fix them," she tapped. "But me. . .I rather like the morning. Everything looks a little clearer. As if there is no limit to how high I can dream."

She realized she was sharing something entirely too personal for a man she'd only met once. Yet it didn't feel wrong to do so. In fact, she suspected she could tell Truman anything. But only time would tell if that were true. Time, and she hoped, lots more games of Taps.

"You win this time. . .I'm tired and getting whimsical, as you can tell. So I better tap out for now." The keys paused beneath her fingers as she wondered if he could feel her drawing back the reins on what she was willing to share about herself.

Knew I'd like you the minute you marched in. You're a gracious loser. Stop. Best of all, you had that I'm-here-to-stay look. Stop. Thanks for coming to Julesberg, Sayra. Stop. Needed someone with a little gumption. Stop. And I'm very pleased to meet you. Stop.

The sincerity of his words rushed through Sayra like honey melting over a hot biscuit. She yawned, rubbed her eyes, and wondered if she could make it through another shift without any sleep.

Ben just rode up over at the livery, Truman informed her. *Guess I'd better tap out for now. Close the office for a few hours. Eat and get some sleep. Can't tell you how long this is gonna take us to repair, so you might have to endure a few more nights of keeping me company, if you don't mind. Who knows, maybe by the time we return, you'll know me better than I know myself . . .better than I want you to.*

six

When Truman signaled Sayra that he would like to play Taps the next night, she battled dueling emotions—curiosity to know more about him and uncertainty because of his last statement over the wire when they'd tapped out at dawn, *who knows, maybe by the time we return, you'll know me better than I know myself . . .better than I want you to.*

*Better than I want you to. . .Better than I want you to. . .*kept pelting her thoughts like a melting icicle's slow, consistent drip. Was he more than he seemed?

Curiosity overruled her uncertainty, and Sayra reminded herself that she could always tap out if she became too uncomfortable with the game. She signaled him to start.

Let me tell you about the time I rode the Pony Express and got into trouble for trying to outrun Bill Cody. . . .

Sayra sensed the man was lonely for companionship and needed a friend simply to listen. Since she'd known him, all he'd done was work. Did he ever take time to relax, play, simply talk face-to-face with anyone? Or was it only over a wire, miles apart from his listener?

When he finished, she shared a tale from her past, enjoying the memories he evoked. She told all about her and Bess's childhood, the happy times with her parents, the wonder of her niece and nephews. For every story she related, he one-upped her with a tale of

wild antics—antics that revealed an open rebellion
against the life his parents had mapped out for him.

My family's been long entrenched in the military, he
explained. *I was Father's only child. He expected me
to become a general, like him and his father and his
grandfather before him. But I wanted no part of the
War between the States. Instead, I joined Edward
Creighton's Western Union crew and headed west—
mainly because I wanted to make certain I was part of
bringing people together through communication.
You've probably guessed communication is important
to me.*

As well she learned. For every night of the remainder of the week, Truman tapped in and the game continued. They told each other of childhood discoveries,
favorite this or that, learned what the other wanted from
life and how he or she planned to achieve those dreams.
Deeper, more difficult truths were shared near week's
end, as if they had latched onto a lifeline and each knew
the other would pull it in safely.

In the first hours of the Saturday shift, when night
had not yet given way to dawn and she had not heard
from him all evening, Truman finally tapped in. *Had
a scattering of business. Nothing that'll stir my
banker's pulse, but steady enough to keep me hopping.
Sorry I couldn't get back to you sooner.*

She missed him. Missed his good humor, as well as
his blatant honesty about his past. "Good to hear your
voi—tap." Sayra giggled. "Or whatever we call this
connection between us." This connection was more
than just words over a wire, she realized. It had become all that had been shared between them. "I waited

and waited and worried that you wouldn't get to talk to me until tonight."

It's been a long time since a woman's waited for me. I think I like that very much, Sayra.

Though she had no right to feel it, a thread of envy untwined itself within Sayra, unfurling through every part of her. Did he court someone along his route? "Meaning there once was a woman who waited for you?" Her fingers moved of their own accord. Had she actually sent the question she voiced aloud?

My wife. She died. Stop.

The silence of the keys sounded so final, Sayra didn't know what to say. Though the envy should have become compassion, Sayra discovered that it took on a heavier twine—jealous—and she was surprised at its intensity. *Thou shall not covet,* she reminded herself sternly, *and you hardly know the man.* Searching for the right words to offer Truman and to regain her composure, she decided to let her heart speak for itself. "I'm sorry I reminded you of your grief. I lost my parents a few years ago, so I know how difficult it is to speak of such things."

It was a long time ago. Ginny and I were very young. She'd been unhappy here and left me several times. Each time I convinced her to return, promising her I would try harder to please her. But Ginny never gave up her desire to head back East until the last time I went after her.

"Is that when she died?" Sayra tapped softly.

Drowned while crossing a river into Kansas.

Sympathy welled in Sayra's eyes. From what she'd learned of Truman Taylor this past week, she suspected he would not allow himself tears. So she shed them for him, offering a prayer that the Lord would soothe his hurt.

Why did she run, Sayra? God knows I need to know why she wouldn't give me a chance.

Silence grew too easily between them, like the quiet just before a storm. How could she advise him when she'd elected to run with Lily without knowing if she'd given Ulysses enough opportunity to deal with the situation concerning her? "Are you a Christian, Truman?"

Why?

"Being one has given me great peace when I'm troubled, and particularly when grief overwhelms me at times."

I want to be one, Sayra. I tried to be one once. I'm just not sure I can be one anymore.

"I'll help you, Tru," Sayra tapped. "We'll help each other." Something new coursed through her. An awareness she had never experienced before. Sayra could hear everything. The tick of the ormolu clock. The jingle of reins on a teamster's wagon outside. The slosh of water being thrown out an upper window of the hotel.

She greeted the first ray of light as it shone on the best day of her life. And perhaps it would prove even better. . .for this day brought the dawn of what she hoped would become a long and abiding friendship between herself and Truman. The thought made her smile.

I've never talked so easily with anyone in my entire life. Thank you, Sayra.

It seemed as if he towered over her now, looking down in her eyes, touching her gently. "Nor have I," she admitted, wishing the keys were his hands and she could know whether they were strong, firm, or calloused. "But surely you and Ginny shared talks like this, didn't you?"

Abrupt clicks answered like continuous slaps against her cheek. Sayra's smile faded, ebbing into a knot of tension that made it difficult to swallow. Refusing to listen, she pressed her hands against her ears. But the harsh rap of the keys seeped into her consciousness, making it impossible to ignore Truman's sudden anger.

"Ginny shared few things with me. Said I was too married to the telegraph to love anything or anyone else. And she was right, Sayra. Still is, for that matter. What happened this week was a game that got carried away. I'm not saying that I'm sorry I made a friend or that I didn't enjoy hearing all about you. Remembering all those things I did as a child reminded me I haven't put any "play" into my life lately. I haven't even had time to visit the Lord's house, I've been so busy working. But Sayra, talk's all it was. . .all it could ever be. We're probably just exhausted. His fear of getting close again erupted along the keys. *If we were face-to-face, I wonder if it would be so easy to say all that we did to one another. Don't make more of this than there is.*

Tears welled and brimmed in her lashes. "Why are you doing this? Our lives have not been so different that we can't at least be friends. Really, I'm sorry I said anything about your wife. I won't again, if you prefer it that way."

Friends, Sayra? Is that all you felt pass between us?

His question left her speechless. So much more had taken seed in her heart during the past few days. More than she dared dream possible. But she was afraid to trust those feelings. Afraid the bond that had formed between them might not hold up to the broad light of day, just as he'd said himself, when life could be seen more clearly.

And truth was, the fear that she might disappoint him in some way and a dread that he'd think her wrong in separating Lily from Ulysses, prevented her from telling him all.

Can't answer? Stop. That's what I thought. Stop. Badger Springs out.

"Truman, wait! Please. . ." She tapped out message after message, but no reply came. Had he left, or was he sitting there listening, ignoring her plea? Sayra stared at the machine, wishing it could somehow transfer her rather than her words to Badger Springs.

The hum started low then built to an angry buzz, like a horde of bees protecting their honeycombs. *Look at our game for what it was. Stop. You're a lonely woman being kind to an even lonelier man. Stop. It can end right there. Stop. Let's just let it go and forget what we told one another, all right?*

Unable to halt the tears that wetted her anger and spilled down her face, Sayra answered his demand with one of her own. "Do you think I'm that shallow? That I would share my deepest secrets with just any man? What kind of woman was your Ginny that she would want to hurt you so?"

If I knew that, she'd be alive. Stop. Doesn't that tell you enough? Stop.

"No, it doesn't. I want to know everything about you, Truman."

Why?

"Because you're the first man I could really care about." Her admission came as a shock to Sayra. As the realization grew in her heart and sprouted into reality, she began to vocalize all the many reasons he intrigued her.

"Because you believe in the same things I do, even once shared the same love of God that I do and might do so again. The fact that you couldn't steal that piece of candy from the emporium tells me you're an honorable man. I know you're dedicated, and unwilling to disappoint anyone. The fact that you rode directly to Badger Springs at the first sign of trouble proves that. And—" she refused to give him the wire, her strokes tapping quicker than his. "Stop right there. Is anyone else you know perfect? No? Then why expect it of yourself? Forgive yourself, Truman. You said she was already dead before you reached her. I'm sure Ginny forgave you."

His message intermixed with her own, garbling both. Finally, Sayra conceded and allowed him the key.

She died because of me. Stop. Time for Ben's shift. Stop. Going to go have a cup of coffee I didn't have to make. Stop. Suggest you do the same. Stop. Get some rest and breakfast. Stop.

"But I'm not finished talking," Sayra insisted. "Remember the game was supposed to last until we both got tired of talking."

I know of only ten commandments, Miss Martin. Stop. Every other rule is subject to change. Stop. Badger Springs operator, out.

seven

The day passed slowly for Sayra. Dedicated to doing a good job for the Western Union, she became frustrated with the minor mistakes she'd made all afternoon.

Near five o'clock, she locked the office door and hung out a sign saying the telegraph would be closed for an hour, then curled up under a blanket on the cot. It seemed she had only closed her eyes when a steady pounding woke her.

"Miss Martin? Sayra? You awake?"

Benjamin Balou's voice sounded like music to a deaf woman. Exhaustion filled every bone in Sayra's body, but she managed to throw off the covers, brush the wrinkles from her skirt and shirtwaist, and anchor a wayward curl behind her ear. "Just a minute," she announced. "Let me unlock it."

A glance at herself in the mirror in her valise assured her she looked presentable. Quickly she unlatched the lock and turned over the closed sign to let everyone know she was once again open for business.

"I'm so glad to see you, Mr. Balou!" she declared, instantly aware of the lines of exhaustion that etched his face. "You look as if you could use some sleep, too."

Ben took off his hat and followed her over to the stove, thanking her when she handed him a cup of coffee.

"It's a few hours old," she apologized, "but if you'd like, I can make a fresh pot." She waved him to the chair opposite hers at the desk.

He sipped the hot brew, then exhaled a deep sigh. "No, that's all right. I can make it. Tru and I took the same schedule we normally work, so all I'm tired from is the ride here. He said to make sure you got some rest just as soon as I rode in. Jubilee says he's feeling fit enough to sit up now, and he might as well be sitting up in the telegraph shack. Mrs. Jube said if Tru would give them 'til Sunday morning, she'd set up housekeeping right there in that tent, and Tru could come on back and get his own self some rest."

Sayra started to protest about making Ben start two hours early, but he insisted she follow Truman's orders. "And you're going to take most of tomorrow off, too. You missed church last Sunday, and you don't look like the sort of lady who misses often. You're not going to miss services tomorrow."

Offering him a smile of gratitude, Sayra stood and gathered her things. "You're right, Ben. I don't, and I really appreciate your letting me have the privilege."

The bell over the door jangled. In walked Lily, looking bright-eyed and eager. "Good morning, Aunt Sayra. Good to see you, Ben." She waited politely as greetings were exchanged, then rushed up and grabbed her aunt's valise. "Major Quinton had breakfast this morning at Mrs. Koumalapalous's. He's invited us to a picnic after church services tomorrow. Since Mr. Ben's here, maybe we can tell Parker yes? Pleeease?"

Hiding a yawn behind her palm, Sayra started to decline. But the gentle pleading etching her niece's lovely face reminded her that she'd been so busy with work, she hadn't had time to offer Lily. Lily had spent much of her first week alone in Julesberg—alone, except for the company of Major Quinton. Perhaps chaperoning the first outing away from the settlement would be a wise decision.

"Tell him that would be lovely," Sayra conceded, thinking it would be pleasant to see some of the surrounding countryside. All she'd seen of Julesberg, Colorado, were these four walls and her room at the boarding house. "But you'll have to help me prepare the food. I'm not sure what Mrs. Kou has handy, but I'm hopeful—"

"He said, all we have to do is bring our pretty faces and our parasols, if we like." Lily rocked back on her heels, pleased with her aunt's agreement. "Major Quinton said we'd have chicken and sweet potato pie. And some of Sergeant York's camomile tea. Oh, and Mrs. Kou said she'd make him some of that corn salad we both like and a dozen of those sourdough biscuits she makes every morning. We don't have to cook a thing!"

Sayra laughed, catching a measure of Lily's enthusiasm. A deep sigh escaped her. "Relaxing and eating a good meal sounds very appealing, love. Thanks for thinking of it." She gave her niece a gentle hug.

"Aunt Sayra, you're going to just love Parker," Lily announced.

A look of caution passed from Ben to Sayra as she glanced over her niece's head at her replacement and replied, "I'd like to get to know him a little better first."

❧

Afternoon sun beat down upon Sayra, prickling her skin first with heat, then with a slight chill from the breeze that had kicked up. With a bit of surprise, she realized she'd dozed off sitting against the tree trunk. Her eyes jerked opened instantly, sensing something amiss.

A quick scan revealed the major had stretched out on the blanket several yards away, using the now empty picnic basket as a headrest. He was dozing as well. The last thing she remembered was her niece's pleasant soprano filling the cove with the voice of an angel. The notes had given Sayra a feeling of peace, lulling her into a relaxation she hadn't felt for days. Now, Lily was nowhere to be seen.

Sayra didn't wait. Running toward the bank near the small cove, she checked the area for signs of Lily. Her niece loved to take off her shoes and wade in water, but she wasn't near the water's edge. Sayra checked upstream and downstream aways but found nothing.

Major Quinton rolled over and pushed his hat up from his eyes. "Problem?"

"Lily's wandered off." Sayra tried to keep the worry from her tone. She had to think clearly, calm herself. "She loves wildflowers. Perhaps she's gone off to gather some from that little patch we passed up the hill. It's turning cold; I think we ought to start back for town as soon as possible."

He rose immediately. "You go see if she's picking flowers. I'll take a further look up and down the stream. If you haven't spotted her in an hour come back. You can take a buggy into town and get help, and I'll keep looking. Maybe George Gaines, the rancher who owns this property, will come by soon, and I'll enlist his help. He usually makes a trip into town on Sundays. We might catch him on the way back."

Sayra agreed that the plan was wise, then headed up the hill toward the team, her worry for Lily growing. Her niece became so entranced with the world and its beauty, she often lost track of time. If Lily got lost, Sayra would never forgive herself.

Grabbing her shawl from the seat where she'd left it inside the buggy, Sayra walked toward the copse of cottonwood trees she remembered sheltering the wildflower meadow. Wind rustled the leaves, making them look like flickering green fire. She wrapped the shawl around her and whispered a prayer that the day would remain sunny, but she couldn't shake the feeling that the weather was just beginning to brood.

Trees soon gave way to wild berry bushes and brambles she hadn't noticed from the road. She turned this way and that, glancing backward occasionally to make certain she hadn't lost her direction. "Lily!" she called time after time, each yell becoming louder, until her throat stung from shouting, "Lily Van Buren, you answer me!"

White puffballs of milkweed swirled around her, dancing upon the air currents. The temperature became another concern, promising to grow colder as night approached. Sayra could feel her nose and cheeks tighten. Her fingers began to tingle from the chill. Wildflowers bent and swayed all around her, dusting her with heady perfume. Still, no sign of Lily.

Sayra pressed her hand over her eyes, peering into the distance, wondering how far the meadow stretched. What if she'd guessed wrong? Where else could Lily have gone?

Something caught her attention. To the left, a wooden

structure. A shack or barn, perhaps. Had Lily taken refuge there?

Running as fast as her legs would carry her, Sayra welcomed the rush of heat that coursed through her because of the movement, keeping the chill at bay even for a few minutes. She reached the shack and pressed her back against it. Her lungs felt as if they would burst from her chest, until finally her breath no longer came in rapid gasps and her heartbeat slowed to its normal rhythm.

Fortune shone on her, for the door to the barn opened freely. Sudden stillness pressed against her chilled skin, the air heavy with dust, aging leather, and hay. "Lily?" she asked, hoping to see her niece's beloved face or hear her sweet voice.

Nothing.

Forcing panic down her throat, she moved into the dim light. Sunlight filtered through cracks in the planked walls. Stalls, reeking with the scent of long-ago animals, now stood empty but for outdated saddles and riggings. Hay still lined the floors and the loft overhead. Riding whips and lariats, tools of every sort, hung on the walls. All looked as ancient as the barn walls themselves. If Gaines owned the barn, he must be a wealthy man, indeed, to let so many things go idle. She would make certain she called upon him about Reverend Simmons's request for funds or wood for additional pews.

"Lily?" She took another step. Without the wind, the freezing air drifted silently around her, sending goose bumps across her skin.

Something moved and raced toward her. Sayra jumped to one side, clamping her hands over her mouth

to stifle a scream. She thought she heard a giggle.
"Lily?"

The shadow took shape. Beady eyes glared at her.
Pointed teeth flashed, then disappeared as the furry
beast scampered away. A shudder quaked through
Sayra. A rat! Big as the length of her foot. Her mind
registered the creature now hid from her, but that didn't
stop her heart from pounding nor keep her from gaug-
ing the distance between the danger of the barn and
the safety beyond the door.

Forcing herself to relax, she realized there might be
many of God's creatures lurking in the countless ha-
vens the barn offered. Every nook and cranny could
give lodging to any type of rodent, insect, snake, or
varmint that could crawl its way under the slatted
planks that formed the barn's walls. Sayra grabbed the
pitchfork resting against the door and silently dared
the rat to charge her again. She didn't have it within
her to kill the monstrous beast, but she could certainly
frighten it away, if need be.

The only way to find Lily was to continue searching. Perhaps she had fallen asleep as well. Now, where
would she choose to lie down? Sayra wondered, looking at all the opportune places. Her eyes focused on a
huge bearskin coat which hung on a nail by the ladder
leading to the loft. A beaver hat hung next to it. She
quickly donned the garment, ignoring the dust that
sprinkled generously to the floor as she wrapped
herself in its warmth. Deciding to protect her hair from
the wind on their way back to the buggy, Sayra
knotted her wind-tangled hair underneath the hat and
settled it upon her head.

Her shoulder bumped a ladder. Instinctively, her eyes focused on the loft. Filled with hay, it would provide a comfortable mattress to lie on. Would Lily have considered this? Just as Sayra lifted one foot to climb the rung of steps leading upward, the door she'd come through earlier swung open, allowing a blast of cold air to enter.

If she and Lily had to spend the night here while waiting out the storm, she'd best close the door more securely to keep out as much of the cold as possible. A high-pitched squeak behind her made Sayra swing around and stab at the air with the pitchfork.

Fingers suddenly closed around both her arms, biting into her skin like clamps of cold iron—fingers strong enough to crush her if she resisted.

Like a sand doll emptied of its stuffing, blood seemed to drain from Sayra. She jerked away, trying to get as far from the attacker as possible. With a sudden, violent tug the man pulled her back, twisting her around.

"Let me go!" she demanded, her heart pounding wildly, as if it might explode from her chest.

"What are you planning to do with that pitchfork?" he demanded, his voice raspy and gruff from the cold.

She became as motionless as the rat, praying with all her soul that there was a way to escape.

Hay fell from above landing on Sayra's head. The urge to sneeze overtook her, but she wiggled her nose and tried to resist.

"Sayra?"

Surprise in the man's voice made it recognizable. The identity of her attacker took shape and substance. "Major Quinton? Why did you grab me?"

"I saw you run into the barn, then all I could see once I entered was a man climbing up the ladder with a pitchfork in one hand. I guess I thought the wors—"

A loud crack rent the air.

A look of surprise filled the soldier's face before he crumpled at Sayra's feet.

Behind him stood Lily with a plank of wood gripped in her hand. Tears burst from her eyes as she apologized, "I didn't recognize him, Aunt Sayra. All I saw was a man attacking you. I couldn't let him hurt you. I had to hit him. I didn't want to, but I had to. You didn't do anything bad to him. People shouldn't hurt you when you're not bad, should they, Aunt Sayra? Please, please don't be angry with me."

Sayra grabbed her niece and hugged her fiercely. "I'm not angry with you, Lily. You've done nothing wrong. It's just that neither did he." She quickly explained that the major thought she was a man attacking them with a pitchfork.

Though she reassured Lily there would be no blame placed on either of them, a closer inspection revealed the major was badly hurt. He wasn't moving. His breath was shallow at best. "We've got to get him into town, or Major Quinton might die," she informed Lily. "He's losing a lot of blood."

"I'll go get the team," the girl volunteered. "I can find my way back easily."

"No," Sayra insisted, listening to the whistle and whine of the wind. "There's nothing we can do for him here. We'll both go. I don't want us separated for any reason."

Sayra took the bandanna from around Major

Quinton's neck and wadded it up into a ball, placing it over his head wound. She took off the bearskin coat and draped it around Lily, warning her to grip her hand at all times. "Don't let go, no matter what. It's getting dark, and I don't want us lost in this."

More than thirty minutes later they'd managed to find the buggy and calm the team enough to maneuver them toward the barn. Getting Major Quinton lifted into the buggy's seat proved the monumental task, for his limp body was far too heavy for both women. After a great deal of struggle, however, they managed.

Making certain Lily was nestled in one side, with the soldier propped between them, Sayra took the reins and urged the horses into a trot. "Get us back in time," she prayed openly, listening to the plod of the horse's hooves against prairie loam. When they finally reached the roadway, she bent her head to the wind and hurried the team into a gallop.

The top of the buggy prevented Sayra from seeing much of the overcast clouds, but she smelled the first touch of winter in the biting cold. Wind scalded her cheeks. Frosty air swirled around them, urging Sayra to huddle close. If only it would not snow until they reached town.

Snatching an occasional glance at their patient and Lily, Sayra began to worry in earnest. Lily clutched the coat tightly around her, but her body shivered like the cottonwood leaves Sayra had seen earlier. And her niece's teeth were chattering. Sayra had quit quaking minutes ago, her skin too numb to feel the cold any longer. Major Quinton looked as if death rode with him—a fact that did little to appease the dread coursing through Sayra's blood like an icy current.

Faith, Sayra reminded herself with each plod of the horses' hooves, *a mustard seed of faith is all you need.*

"D-Do you r-reckon the commander will put me in jail for h-hitting Major Quinton?" Lily asked, her eyes rounded like saucers.

Sayra straightened her back, forcing herself to keep her grip on the reins as tightly as she could. Days with too little sleep and the effort of lifting the major had weakened her stamina. "You'll not go to jail. I'll see to that. Even if we have to leave Julesberg."

"Oh, I hope we don't leave, Aunt Sayra. I like Mrs. Koumalapalous very much." Lily pressed a hand on Sayra's arm.

Concern spiraled through her. Her niece's fingers were like ice. "Put your hands inside your skirt pockets. That will keep them warmer. Look. . ." Hope raced through Sayra as she realized the mustard seed had taken root. "I can see the lights of town, Lily. Look there! It can't be more than a mile or two."

A grin spread across Lily's face as she stuffed her hands inside her pockets. "We made it, Aunt Sayra. You can do just about anything! Do you think everyone will forgive us for hurting Major Quinton?"

A deep sigh of relief escaped Sayra's lips in a puff of frosty air. One more blessing seemed a small thing to ask for. "With God's help, anything's possible, Lil."

eight

Sayra keyed in the final word and stared at Benjamin with regret in her eyes.

"He's going to want to know why." Ben pointed at the telegraph machine as it began to tick off dots and dashes furiously. "I told you. You can't just up and quit. He suspects there's more than you're telling him. Why *are* you and Lily leaving, Sayra?"

She stared at the key, watching the wire hum with Truman's demand for an answer, knowing she owed him more of an explanation, but unwilling to put into words the real reason for her resignation. Her palms splayed open near her shoulders, as if someone had yelled, "Hands up!" and she were being robbed of more than the place she'd hoped to call home. "Tell him I couldn't say anything more. That's the truth. Besides, if we don't catch the stage, there won't be another until next week."

If only she hadn't received Ulysses' wire this afternoon, demanding that she return home with Lily. If not, he intended to come out on the next stagecoach.

At least he was willing to take time away from his precious work to fetch his daughter, but Sayra suspected it was simply Ulysses' pride that had been hurt, not that he felt any real need to protect Lily. He hadn't said a single thing about resolving the reason they'd left Port Hudson in the first place.

The best thing to do was move on so Lily wouldn't

be so accessible to her father. . .if he carried his threat through. Once more time had passed, and the telegraphers back home let her know the "woman order" had been lifted, then she would gladly take Lily home.

A glance around the office made Sayra aware of how much she'd grown fond of the place. "I'll never forget Julesberg, Ben. Nor you or Truman. Forgive me for leaving you with it all."

With an abrupt turn, Sayra hurried outside. The jingle of the bell over the door mixed with the click, clickety-click of the telegraph, keeping time with the ache that pounded at her temples.

"Aunt Sayra, you ready to go?" Lily rose from the bench just outside the office. "The stage reined in over at the livery, and the driver said he'd be pulling out in fifteen minutes. That was a few minutes ago. I went ahead and let them stow our baggage."

Sayra looked at her niece's red-rimmed eyes and felt her heart clutch at the unfairness of the situation. Lily had made friends here, especially with Mrs. Kou.

But they had to move on now. Once Ulysses arrived and learned of the incident with Major Quinton, he would surely attempt to convince Bess that Sayra was incapable of caring for Lily properly, pointing out that Lily was learning habits unbecoming to a Van Buren. The small thread of reason that allowed Bess to let Lily go with Sayra would surely fray and bend in Ulysses' favor.

❧

As the driver cracked his whip, the coach rattled and swayed, bouncing along the rutted road at a breakneck speed toward the next of many stage stations. A kaleidoscope of prairie rushed by, fogged in dust kicked up beneath the team's hooves. Sayra closed her eyes against the oppressive heat captured in such close quarters, her teeth rattling with each jostle of the coach.

The cold front that had blown in last night had rushed south like bad gossip. Perspiration now dampened Sayra's skin in a sheen that threatened to stain her dress irreparably. She yearned for even the slightest breeze. Her left arm ached from being in one position for hours, but Lily pressed her cheek against it as she slept. Sayra didn't have the heart to move and disturb her. Discomfort, exhaustion, and the lack of air got the better of her temperament, causing Sayra's faith to leave her for a moment.

Why can't we find peace, Lord? she wondered, staring at the strangers who shared the coach. *Are they more deserving than Lily and me? Am I taking us to happiness, or will this be just another stopping place?* Sayra believed everything that happened brought learning to one's life, but at what point was peace to be experienced?

"How much farther, is it, Aunt Sayra?" Lily murmured, her lashes opening to reveal tired, blue-violet eyes. "I need to stretch."

"Not far, Sweet." She pulled a hanky from her reticule and offered it to Lily. "Wipe your face and neck. I wetted it back at the last station, but I'm afraid it's no longer damp."

Not far, indeed. Sayra's concern sped through her thoughts. Their money was almost as depleted as their patience and good humor. Though she still had part of the funds Truman advanced her, it wouldn't be enough to survive on if she didn't find employment almost immediately.

But she knew nothing of the small encampment the stageline clerk back at Julesberg called Honor's Glory. Probably one of those mining camps that sprang up overnight wherever gold was discovered, then disappeared within three to five years. Sayra only knew the encampment was as far as her ticket would take them until she earned enough to pay Truman Taylor the debt she owed him. Then she would save until she could settle in a larger town, like Denver.

"Honor up ahead!" The driver's announcement whipped through the open-air window, dust billowing the oilcloth curtains that attempted to keep the passengers protected from the weather. He urged the team into a faster gait.

As if they sensed they would soon be replaced by a fresh team, the horses leaned into their traces, making the coach lunge forward. The driver complimented the three perfectly matched pairs, promising them fresh oats and a good brushing down if they improved his best speed record for the last five miles.

The land rose steeply, causing the coach to lean with it. Sayra and Lily held onto one another. Glancing out their window, Sayra suggested they focus on a safer vista. The stagecoach traveled a winding road uphill, hugging the mountain on one side, missing a yawning chasm on the other by less than five feet.

"Don't look." Lily held Sayra tightly against her. "You know how you dislike heights, Aunt Sayra. Heaven must be somewhere near here, 'cause this sure looks high to me."

Prayers were such odd opportunities. Some were for important things like asking for your life to be whole again. Others were given to someone else, offering sincere wishes that a friend or loved one's life would be blessed. But the prayer that passed through Sayra's lips was purely and simply relying on faith—faith that this coach would reach its destination with everyone intact.

The ride was harried as the team carried them higher and higher toward the steep, craggy peaks of the Rocky Mountains. Five miles of climbing uphill felt like twenty on level ground. Sayra thought the ride would never end, until finally the coach seemed to dip backward. The osage wheels groaned as the team's gait slowed from gallop to trot. When the driver reined in and the coach halted in a flurry of dust, leather straps beneath the coach creaked and bowed like arthritic bones.

"At last," Lily announced and straightened, relieving Sayra of the pressure on her arm.

Sayra waited while the male passengers disembarked. With a forefinger, she moved the curtain aside enough to see the settlement that would be her and Lily's new home. Squinting through the cloud of dust that still hovered over the stagecoach, she blinked away the image.

"I'm seeing things." She peered harder. "Tents!" A sea of canvas stretched before her on both sides of the streets. "Not a wooden building in sight!"

Lily was helped out of the coach by one of the men who had ridden with them from Julesberg. Once outside, she turned this way and that, her eyes lit up with pure anticipation. "Oh, Aunt Sayra, you should see it. It looks like a great big Chittauqua. Rows and rows of tents. I wonder if there are any acrobats and lion tamers inside?"

Accepting a hand from the driver, Sayra stepped down onto the dusty street and realized there weren't even any planked sidewalks. No telegraph lines graced the skyline. Disappointment filled her instantly, sinking like a lure into the pit of her stomach. No telegrapher's job here.

Only one building had been crudely constructed of clapboard. Over its false front, the words *Honor's Glory Bank and Trust* had been painted. On the front glass window, one of the few new looking items the town boasted, a sign indicated a doctor was in residence. It seemed appropriate the two shared a business, Sayra decided. That way the doctor always got paid.

"Is there a hotel or boarding house?" She stared aghast down the narrow lane that divided the settlement in half. While the city of tents made up either side of the roadway, workings of mines scattered the countryside as it rose to join the upward thrust of the Rockies. "Or a church?"

Lily leaned a bit closer. "Wouldn't Jimmy Don just love this? It looks like a giant revival meeting. You know how he loves listening to all those circuit preachers."

Homesickness swept through Sayra at Lily's mention of her youngest nephew. Bess would be sitting on the porch in her rocker, darning socks or quilting for the coming winter. The boys would be out in the yard, chasing chickens or pestering each other. Ulysses was probably pulling into the yard at this very moment. . .

The thought of her brother-in-law brought Sayra back to the troubles at hand. They must find a place to stay and employment as soon as possible. But where. . .on both accounts?

"Give you ladies a hand?" A body moved through the passengers and started grabbing the baggage being tossed down from the top of the coach.

It was hard to say what Sayra noticed first about him. Maybe it was the way he handled the heavy luggage as if it were nothing but bales of feathers. Or perhaps it was the layers of clothing the man chose to wear. Knee-high boots aged by the wear and tear of years rather than months. Buckskins whose fringe had been lightened various shades, no doubt by the countless washings, she supposed, while still on his body. The leggings and arms fit the wiry man like a second skin, tailored to his every move. Dark, rich fur that seemed more cape than coat billowed behind him, giving the stranger a look of wilderness royalty.

But it was the shock of an occasional glimpse of glacial-blue eyes and ermine-colored hair beneath the man's slouch hat that caused Sayra to continue looking.

"Goodness, Aunt Sayra, isn't he the most unusual man you've ever seen?" Lily stared, open mouthed at their helper.

"Name's Aud," the man informed, handing each belonging to its owner. His voice was gravelly-sounding but softer than his appearance led one to anticipate. "Aud Williams. Owner of the *It'll Do Mine* up on

Widow's Peak. And you?"

Sayra remembered her manners and introduced themselves. "We would be much obliged, Mr. Williams, if you would show us to the nearest lodgings."

Aud stared off into the direction of the tents. "Don't guess there's much place for a lady to stay. 'Leastways, your kind of lady." He turned and eyed them from head to hem. "You are Christian women, ain't ya?"

Both Lily and Sayra assured him they did their best to be.

"That's what I figured. You ain't gonna find nothing but sin and trouble in Honor's Glory. I'd be to lighting out of here when the stage leaves."

Sayra picked up her valise and one end of their trunk, instructing Lily to grab the other end. "We'll be staying, Mr. Williams. Much obliged for your help."

"You don't listen well, do you, lady?" Aud waved his arm at the rest of the passengers who had gathered luggage and now strolled toward individual destinations. "There's reason no females but you two got off here in Honor. It ain't the sort of place you try to hang a petticoat. This is a rough camp, full of mean, vile, wicked souls. Men who think women are a bad omen unless they're plying a trade older than mining. A regular Sodom and Gomorrah, it is. You ladies *can't* stay. There ain't no jobs open, except those up in the. . . ," his voice lowered so Lily couldn't hear, "crib district. Though I'd guess there are a couple a choices a year or two younger than your sister, there."

"She's my niece," Sayra informed, "and we're willing to cook, clean, or wait tables if necessary." Desperation began to fill her as Sayra realized she might have taken them to the ends of the earth with no way to get back. *"Decent* jobs.*"*

"Like I said, ma'am. Hard as it may sound," the miner pulled up the buckskin gloves that covered his surprisingly small hands, "There's no place for a regular kind of female here."

The jingle of the reins being gathered up and the driver's last call for Georgetown made Sayra panic. "When will the next stage for Denver arrive?"

Aud stepped over and tapped a document pinned to the tent that housed the livery animals. "Says here a week from Thursday. . .that's if the pass don't get muddied or snowed in. Then it could be weeks, maybe even months."

She watched in horror as the driver flicked his team into motion and the stagecoach that had been their harried haven for days rode away, taking with it seemingly every semblance of civilization.

"What are we going to do, Aunt Sayra?" Lily asked innocently. "We don't have enough savings to wait for the next stage. We've got to find some kind of work."

Piercing blue eyes focused on one pair of violet pools, then the other. "You two came as far as your money would take you, didn't ya?"

Embarrassment flamed Sayra's cheeks. "The Lord will provide a way."

A grin stretched across Aud's face, flashing rows of surprisingly even, white teeth. "You know, I like that, Sister. I never thought of myself as a 'mysterious way,' but I reckon that is downright appealing."

Sayra protested as he took the heavy trunk from them and manhandled it into a wagon hitched one tent away.

"What are you doing?"

Aud tipped back the slouch hat sheltering the blue of his eyes. "You know that hymn that says the Lord works in mysterious ways?"

"I do!" Lily proclaimed proudly.

"I'll just bet you do, Little Miss." Aud offered a hand for Lily to step up into the driver's box. "Well, I'm one of His mysterious ways, today, 'cause I'm fixin' to take you two Christians home with me. I need me a house-keeper and a cook. Y'all done got yourself a job."

"But we don't know you," Sayra objected.

"Well, I like him," Lily announced, instantly giving him her trust. "We don't know anyone else here any-way, so we got to work for some stranger. Why not for Mr. Aud?"

Trying to convince Lily, once she made up her mind, was a losing battle for Sayra. She climbed in and took a seat in the back of the wagon with the sacks of supplies the man had gathered from somewhere in the tent city.

Aud hopped up into the seat by Lily, gave her a wink, and flicked the mule team into motion. "Ho, Jenny. There you go, Jack. Got us some company. Now take me to the shack." A chuckle escaped him, and he complimented Lily, "Got me spouting poetry, gal."

As he swung the team out into the roadway and headed up the lane of tents, Aud warned, "You two la-dies just keep a lookin' straight. Don't pay them fellas no never mind. They ain't seen a righteous woman in quite a spell, I suspect, so they'll be a-gawking atcha."

Sure to his word, men stopped whatever they were doing and stared after the muleteam, some pointing at the new women in town.

"Close your ears, Lily," Sayra announced, her face heating to stain her cheeks a deep crimson. Lily did as told and pressed her hands over her ears. Aud spurred the team into a steady gallop, and soon the tents looked like a low horizon of white peaks behind them.

Though she could tell by the miner's kindness and the way he flushed with equal embarrassment at the catcalls several of the men shouted while they passed, Sayra still felt a bit uneasy about depending on a total stranger and his home for their well-being. "I don't mean to be ungrateful, Mr. Williams, but I must take my niece's welfare under consideration. How do we know that you're a God-fearing man of good conscience?"

Aud threw back his head and laughed, a laugh that erupted from the tip of his toes and exited in a whoop that echoed over the mountainside. Lily enjoyed it so much, she started giggling, a pleasant childish sound that warmed Sayra's heart. Suddenly feeling light-hearted herself, Sayra allowed the laughter to bubble within her. Soon all three were a chorus of snickers and snorts. Hoots and yuk-yuks made driving the team impossible.

"Wha-Wha-What's so funny?" Sayra asked, wiping the tears from the corner of one eye. She felt years younger and strangely at peace.

Lily slapped her thigh, her shoulders bobbing up and down like apples at an apple-dunking contest. "You are, Aunt Sayra." She chuckled, hiding a snicker behind her palm.

"Me? How so?"

Aud looked at her niece in anticipation, as if Lily

had surprised him as well.

"'Cause Mr. Aud can't be a God-fearing man of good conscience," Lily snorted. "He's a girl."

Sayra thought it all a joke until she watched the waves of surprise, disbelief, realization, then admiration wash over the miner's face. Lily had spoken the truth. *He* really was a *she!*

"Well, pour salt in my coffee and call it sweet, ain't you about the smartest gal I've ever had the notion of meeting?" Aud took off her glove and offered Lily her hand. "Proud to meet you, Miss. I'm Audrey Williams, from San Antone way."

Lily pumped her hand as if she were priming a water spigot. "Lily Van Buren, of the Port Hudson Van Burens."

"Glad to meet you, Miss Lily. And your aunt?"

"Speechless," Sayra announced. "Just call me plain and simply speechless."

Audrey and Lily burst into another fit of laughter.

nine

"Why don't I believe you?" Truman demanded, leaning over the desk, his green eyes locked into a battle of wills with Major Quinton.

The Western Union man called upon all his willpower to resist the anger racing through him like a salvo of lightning—an anger that would have propelled his fist into the soldier's jaw, if Tru allowed the impulse. Common sense told him the sergeant waiting outside the fort commander's office would lose no time coming to the major's defense. Good judgment and that long game of taps with Sayra last week reminded Truman that he'd headed west to learn less violent ways to seek the truth. Resolving to settle this in a gentlemanly manner, Truman sat in the chair offered to him earlier. "I'd like the whole story, Quinton."

"I've told you what I know. Why would I lie?" The major grimaced as he shifted in his own chair. Though it had only been two days since his injury, he wore no bandage to cover the head wound.

Truman motioned to the hat sitting at an awkward angle on the major's head. "Something tells me you're trying to cover up more than that head wound."

Parker Quinton rose, slamming a fist down on the desk. "I'll hear no more of this. You're impuning my honor, Taylor. I told you all I know. I saw Sayra go into a barn looking for Lily. When I followed her in, it was dark. All I could see was someone in a hat and coat, wielding a pitchfork. My actions were to save the women from an attacker. The moment I realized it was Sayra, someone hit me from behind. I didn't know it was Miss Lily who struck me until the fort commander told me, after I'd regained consciousness." Major Quinton's fist quickly unknotted into a white-knuckled grasp on the desk's edge.

"Sit down before you fall down, man," Truman instructed, pushing his own chair away to rush to the major's aid. The soldier wavered, color draining from his face.

"I'll be fine," Quinton insisted, sinking into the chair and resting his head against the wooden ladderback.

"McDooley!" Truman yelled, "Get in here!"

The door swung open, admitting a small redheaded man dressed in Union blue. "Aye, Tru. . .er. . .Mr. Taylor?"

"You might want to rouse the medic. The major here nearly passed out."

"Right on it, sir—"

"As you are, Sergeant McDooley," Major Quinton's order brought the Irishman to an abrupt halt. "I'll not be needing the medic."

Moving away from the officer, Truman grabbed his hat from the rack near the door. "Suit yourself, Quinton." He placed his hat over his head slowly and deliberately, mulling exactly what he wanted to say. "I know you aren't a churchgoing man. Don't figure you put much stock in the Lord's ways either. But know this. . . ," Truman's eyes narrowed into emerald slits. "If I find out that you're not telling me the truth about what went on in that barn—if those women left

Julesberg because you were less than a gentleman—as God is my witness, you and I will have a reckoning."

"Now, Mr. Taylor, I canna let ye be threatening the major." Sergeant McDooley stepped forward; Truman's tall frame dwarfed the banty rooster of a man. Though McDooley was a mere five foot ten and less than the two hundred pound weight requirement the army demanded—uniform, sabre, survival pack, and all—his deep voice volleyed around the room as if it were faraway thunder rumbling off the mountain peaks.

Truman liked McDooley. Had missed his singing as much as he'd missed church services. The sergeant had one of the finest and loudest baritones in the whole congregation; a pleasant experience, since he was one of the few men in the crowd who could carry a tune. Not that anyone would ever tell him if he didn't, for McDooley was also the best boxing talent in the territory. The Irish leprechaun-sized man had won every match the last two Fourth of July Jubilees.

"I'd appreciate it if you'd stay out of this, Doo." Truman stared down into eyes that no longer held the friendliness he experienced in church. "You and I have no argument. I won't get into fisticuffs with either you or Quinton. You know I gave that up long ago. But there are other ways a man can settle differences, and Major Quinton here needs to know I'll seek them out if he's lying about what happened to the women."

"Escort Mr. Taylor to the door, Sergeant McDooley. This briefing is over."

"Aye, Major."

"I'm leaving. . .for now," Truman announced,

glancing back at the injured man, then at McDooley. A challenge emanated from the rigid stance Tru took, his fists knotted against his hips, his eyes focused and unblinking. Honor kept him from demanding more of Parker Quinton until the man was healthier. Duty bound him to finish the job he'd been paid to do. . .establish a stable telegraph crew here in Julesberg so he could return to Georgetown and all the hundreds of problems going on in the surrounding area.

Sayra's questioning of his Christianity had disturbed him at the most inopportune moments since she'd first reminded him he'd veered far from his faith. Her gentle promise to help him recover his closeness to God rose within him now. He imagined hearing her rhythm on the wire tapping "Do unto others as you would have them do unto you."

Perhaps he should give Quinton the benefit of the doubt.

But a silent promise layered the air with tension between the trio. A promise that Parker Quinton had best be deserving of the doubt and that McDooley should decide if Quinton deserved his loyalty. Because at the first wrong move, the first sign that Quinton had not told the complete truth in this matter, Truman would find it difficult not to allow "an eye-for-an-eye" its literal translation.

"A good day to you, McDooley." Truman respectfully thumbed up his hat to the Irishman, then blatantly turned and offered his back to the officer. "Quinton."

Walking out into the sunlight, Tru made certain his boots sank heavily onto the wood planks that made up the sidewalk leading away from the command post. He slowed, allowing several soldiers to see him as he headed for the livery. That way, no one would suspect his real intent.

Once inside, Tru asked the smithy if he would take a look at his horse. "He was favoring the left front when I rode in. Be back in a few minutes." When the smithy headed down to the stall that housed his pony, Tru made a quick retreat through the back entrance.

Stealthily he made his way past the rows of sleeping quarters and the brig until he finally reached the backside of the officers' quarters. Fortunately, it was morning drill time, and the bulk of the cavalry were in the foreyard drilling. A glance through the barracks' window revealed that the round case where the company kept their weapons was unlocked and empty. That meant a good deal of the regiment was out on early patrol with their commanding officer. He moved past the barracks and crept toward the backside of the command post.

Though Truman disliked the deception, he didn't trust Parker Quinton as far as he could throw his saber. Maybe by listening at the south window that filtered in fresh air to the command office, he would be able to learn something more than he'd been told all morning. Trouble was, standing beneath the pane left Truman in open sight of anyone who might catch him eavesdropping. He would be hard put to explain why he stood there, leaning against the wall with his ear pressed to it.

Truman started to ask the Lord to protect his flank, but it seemed ill-advised when he was doing something so blatantly dishonest. He glanced around for a sign of trouble and found none.

The sun had not yet reached its zenith, leaving a cool shadow on the southern side of the command post.

Wind whipped the curtains out the window, carrying with it a clearly audible conversation. . .thanks to McDooley's boisterous voice.

"Saints and begorra, man! Ye nearly gave yeself away, Major. Mister Taylor isna an ignorant man. He suspects something."

"But truth is on our side. I didn't lie to the man."

"Aye, 'tis true. But neither did ye tell him the whole of it."

A laundress sauntered into view, carrying a basket on one hip. When she spotted Truman, she came to a dead halt, her eyes rounding in fear.

Truman straightened and held a finger to his lips, twisting first one way, then another so she could see that he was unarmed and there would be no gunplay or robbery.

His heart began to hammer against his chest. His pulse drummed in his ears. She held his freedom in her hands as surely as she gripped the basket.

He could almost feel time sifting by as silently as the wind that flowed through the flounces of her skirt. *Please, lady. . .*

The woman shrugged her shoulders and turned away, leaving Truman to his whims.

A great sigh of relief flowed soundlessly from his lips as he once again leaned against the wall, hoping that he had not missed pertinent information.

"We've got to stall for time," Major Quinton insisted. "You know we've got to get those supplies out of there before anyone finds them. If Taylor or Commander Dobbs discovers what we've done, we'll have to head for Mexico."

What a bad stroke of luck, Truman thought. The laundress had made him miss vital information.

"Saddle the horses," Major Quinton instructed. "We'll get things started. Then one or the other of us can check on how it's going every day until we're through. That way we won't raise any suspicion. I'll just tell Corporal Billings I'm heading into town and taking you as escort, since I'm still a bit unsteady in the saddle. He won't question the need for you to accompany me. We'll settle this before Taylor has any idea he's been outfoxed."

"I'm thinkin' ye're underestimating him," the Irishman warned. "Ye best be watchin' ye backside."

"How right you are," whispered Truman as he pushed away from the wall and made his way back to the camp store. "Especially if I find Sayra and Lily and discover you've hurt them in any way."

*

"You're going to hurt yourself doing that," Sayra warned, reminding her niece of what Aud had showed them. "If you insist on panning for this mysterious gold she's trying to find, then bend your knees as Aud said. No sense in breaking your back looking for such nonsense. There's probably as much gold here as there are virtuous women."

She continued to hang laundry on the line she'd strung from the mine shack to the top wire horse-shoeing over the Conestoga.

Aud appeared through the mine entrance at just that moment, squinting her eyes against the brightness of the sun. Her face was smudged with dark earth, dust powdered her shoulder and cap, and her buckskins were stained at the knees, hinting she'd been crawling around for most of the morning.

All of a sudden, she tore into a dead run toward Sayra, yelling at the top of her lungs. "Woman, are you out of your mind?"

Sayra dropped the calico dress she held and threw her hands up to ward off what she believed would be blows. "What's the matter?"

"These!" Aud informed, pulling each pantaloon down and knotting them into a ball. "These are the matter. You'll have every shotgun in the divide down on my head if you start hanging these out to dry near a mine shack. Put those lady things up in the shack somewheres, if you're gonna clean 'em."

Lily and Sayra stood where they were, both shocked by Aud's outburst.

A low rumble of laughter erupted from the miner as she handed Sayra the knot of clothes and swiped off the dust from each of her shoulders. Her nose wrinkled and she sneezed, a half-snort, half-laugh. "Guess I did look like an old buzzard swooping down like you's stealing my best bone, didn't I?"

"I didn't realize hanging up our laundry would offend you, sir. . .ma'am," Sayra apologized, "but I'll see to it we dry them elsewhere. Are you superstitious about where you hang them?"

Her gaze followed Aud's as she took in the sight of Lily panning for gold in the stream that ran alongside the mineshack. Lily, with her hair cascading in long mahogany curls down to her waist. Lily, whose skin had already added a peachy glow to her normally porcelainlike texture. Lily, whose hem was soaked clean up to her knees.

"You know, I forgot what it feels like to wear something so gal-ish." Aud's tone held a whimsical quality.

"I get so caught up in pretending I'm not one, I plum forgot what it's like." She finally turned her attention to Sayra. "As far as being superstitious, I ain't. But plenty of other folks around here are. Same reason I don't wear gal thangs."

Finally, the one question Sayra had been holding back for days might be answered. She had hoped Aud would broach the subject sooner than this, but until now her employer had seemed tight-mouthed about her masquerade.

Glacial blue eyes redirected their focus from Lily to Sayra's inquiring gaze. "Can I trust you, Sayra Martin?"

Aud's frankness took a bit of getting accustomed to, but Sayra found it refreshing. It was an honesty shared by both her employer and her niece and had made the two immediate friends. Could she answer Aud truthfully when she didn't even know if she trusted herself? After all, the only thing she seem to do well was run away.

"I'd like to think you could, Aud."

"I suppose I could tell you, and you'd understand good enough, but look down yonder about forty-five degrees to your right. There's someone who will *show* you why in just a few minutes."

Following the direction Aud's forefinger pointed, Sayra squinted to see what Aud had spotted. "I can't see anything."

"Don't need to see it. Listen."

Lily's attention had been averted from her pan, and she straightened. "Someone's coming. And he's singing. . .something awful."

A frown creased Aud's brow. "You seen Primrose lately?"

Lily pointed toward the shaft. "She followed you into

the mine when you went in."

"Smart skunk. Musta knowed Turk was headin' up this way. Prim and Turk don't get along too good. I figure 'cause he outdoes her in the perfume department, if you know what I mean."

"Turk?" Sayra finally spotted the scarecrow-thin man, riding a mule up the mountainside toward the *It'll Do*.

"Longest neck you ever seen," Aud informed. "Gobbles up food like there's no tomorrow. Makes you want to hide your winter supplies. Still-in-all, he's got a good heart. Can recite the Good Book frontards and backards and would give you the buckskin off his back if you asked him." A grimace bracketed Aud's lips. "Not that you'd want that piece of hide. No telling when's the last time he scrubbed it."

Lily giggled. A brow arched over one of Sayra's eyes, and she took a closer look at Aud.

"Now I know what you're thinking. But at least I fling myself down in the crick once in a while, whether I need it or not. . .clothes and all!"

The seriousness of Aud's tone brought a smile to Sayra's face. In the days she'd spent cooking and cleaning for her new employer, she'd discovered many likeable things about the woman who insisted upon dressing as a man. Honorable things that excused her unconventional ways.

"Ho, the camp!" Turk hollered as the mule topped the last rise before the ground leveled out into the yard in front of the mine shack.

An odor permeated the air, reminding Sayra of "Swap" day in the Port Hudson markets. Trappers from all over the territory brought in pelts of beaver, minx, fox, wolf, and other wilderness prey and swapped them for staples, like flour and sugar, fryback, and coffee sold by Port Hudson merchants. This might very well be one of those men.

"Is that women I see, Aud Williams?" the odorous man asked. "Female women? They ain't been down in the mine, have they?"

"Grab the rest of them frills, Sayra," Aud instructed, moving forward to greet the newcomer, "and get that little gal out of the water 'til I see which side of the post he hangs his hat."

Sayra told Lily to come help her gather the remainder of the laundry.

"Why, that's sure 'nuff two females if'n I ever seen 'em."

Turk's Adam's apple bobbed up and down in his long neck so elaborately, that Sayra knew immediately how he'd earned his name.

He grabbed his hat from his head and bowed low against the mule's mane. "Ma'am. Miss. Name's Jebediah Turkelrod. Most folks call me Turk."

Sayra nodded, while Lily gave a brief curtsey and introduced themselves to him.

"Both misses, huh? Now who'd a thought ol' Aud would up and get hisself two females. Why, the man never once went with me into town. Mabel Annie's been trying to get into his—"

"Miss Martin and Miss Van Buren are my housekeeper and cook," Aud interrupted, taking the reins to the mule while Turk dismounted.

"Housekeeper and cook. Ain't you comin' up in the hills." A look of genuine pleasure crossed his whiskered face. "You mean you got some decent cooking?"

Lily rocked back on her heels. "Aunt Sayra's the best this side of the divide."

Aud laughed. "And Miss Lily's giving me a run for my nuggets, 'cause she's the best panner I ever seen sift the silt."

Turk rubbed his hands together in anticipation, then held them up to his face. "Ooohhhweee, ain't that a nose-pinching smell. Guess I'd better do myself some washing up 'fore you invite me to vittles."

Aud's eyes ovaled into two sapphires as she stared first at the visitor who walked over to the wash barrel and began scrubbing his face and hands, then at Sayra and Lily. "I do believe you two must be guardian angels or some kind of special blessings brung my way."

"Why's that?" Sayra asked, following Aud's gaze as it poured over Turk.

"'Cause frankly, that right there is a downright miracle."

❧

"It's a sin," Turk stated, one side of his cheek bulged out with the half-slice of venison he had forked into it seconds ago. "Females cannot work in the mines."

"Who said so?" No challenge filled Lily's tone, for the question had been asked in all sincerity.

Turk narrowed gray eyes at Aud. "You been talking nonsense to these gals? They think they're going to get to deep earth with the rest of us?"

Aud scooped another mouthful of beans and said around them, "I tol' you nigh on five years now, Turkelrod, ain't nothing wrong with a woman being down in the mine. Ain't no such thing as all that superstitious hogwash. I been planning me a way to prove it to you hardheads, and one a these years blamed if I won't. You just wait and see."

Sayra rose from the table the four of them shared in Aud's mine shack, grabbed the blue-speckled pot of coffee, and poured more into their visitor's cup. "We have no interest in digging for gold, Mr. Turklerod. But I assure you, if we had, we would not let the fact that we were of the female persuasion stop us."

Respect and approval glinted in Aud's eyes, making Sayra proud she'd defended their right. It seemed important to Aud, and she had a pretty good guess why. After all, Aud was doing the very thing Turk said was blasphemous.

"You'll bring down the tommyknockers on us." Turk made the sign of the cross over his face and heart, then knocked three times on the wooden table.

"Lots of the panners around the divide believe it's bad luck to let a woman work in the mines. Says it'll let loose the ghoulies that cause problems under the earth. I say, if you'd spend less time worrying about what can't be done in a mine, you might have more time to do what you aim to be doing there in the first place. One of these days, some gal's gonna prove you all wrong, just to set your thinking straight. Besides, ain't no such thing as ghoulies."

Suddenly Sayra understood completely. Audrey Williams chose to live the life as a man so that, one day, she could rid the other miners of their superstitions. How would they ever deny her capabilities, if she brought in the mother lode and they discovered all this time she was female?

"You act like you ain't got no superstitions," Turk sulked.

"Just one, if you want to call it that," Aud admitted.

"Ever heard of the Sermon on the Mount?"

Lily nodded. "Anyone who's read the Bible has."

"Well, whether you live here in the Rockies or you just got a plain old hill you can ride up on, my superstition is that you'll miss the biggest blessing of your life if you don't give yourself your own sermon on the mount. Some folks do it on Sunday, some other days. I do it every morning the sun shines through my winder. Sometimes even in the snow. You ain't seen God 'til you seen him wake up on Widow's Peak, I'm telling ya. Fact is, if you wanna see what I'm talking about, I can take you there in the morning."

"I'd like to go see God." Excitement filled Lily's face.

"You don't have to, Child," Turk reassured Lily, pressing a hand to his heart. "God's right here, no matter where you go. Didn't you know that?"

A deep sigh escaped Lily and relief washed through her expression. "Good. I didn't know if He could find me; we've been moving around so much."

Sayra felt their attention as it focused solely on her. Leaving Port Hudson and Julesberg had had many repercussions, but she had no idea it had caused Lily's faith to waiver. She didn't need someone to "stone her at the well" to decide she'd been wrong in some of her choices. Pushing away her meal, Sayra asked Lily to reach out her hand.

"You don't have to worry anymore, love," she promised. "Maybe He shouldn't be the one having to track us down. Tomorrow you and I will go find Him again together."

ten

"How much farther?" Lily asked, stopping to take a deep breath.

Sayra wondered the same. Though they hadn't climbed hand-over-foot yet, the path leading to Aud's "church" site was becoming steep and physically taxing.

"Rest a minute." Aud halted a few yards above them. She turned and pointed to a path that led between two boulders. "Just a bit more. I took y'all the easy way around this morning. Didn't want to scare you off. But I guarantee, the sight will be worth the trouble."

As they rested, gray fingers of dawn splayed across the sky, brightening into mauve, orange, then saffron. The surrounding peaks blossomed in panoramic color as sunlight warmed the mountain's face and evaporated the morning mists that rose from the foothills.

Snuggling deeper into her shawl, Sayra was grateful Aud had suggested they wear their heavy serge dresses and poke bonnets to make the climb rather than the calico they might have worn to a regular church service. The clothing helped stave off some of the chill in the air. Aud seemed unaffected, even invigorated by the cold, dressed as she was in her wilderness buckskins and fur cape.

"If we don't get to scrambling now, we'll miss it."

"By all means." Sayra proceeded forward, linking

one arm through Lily's and lifting the bottom of her skirt slightly so the morning dew would not stain its hem quite so much. "Show us the way. I wouldn't want to climb this far for nothing."

Lily seemed more energetic, thriving on the challenge of reaching Widow's Peak before dawn gave way completely to day. Hers was the impatience of youth, wanting to get wherever they were going long before it was possible.

Minutes later Aud disappeared between the two boulders. "Come see! Hurry. It's breaking."

Her voice seemed to echo as if she were in a deep valley, and it reverberated off granite walls. Lily's steps hastened, inspiring Sayra to increase her own gait. Passing through the path between the boulders, Sayra stepped up and realized they had finally reached the top. She blinked once. . .twice. . .her gaze attempting to take in all the magnificence that stretched before her.

Mountain peaks reached for the sky as if they were arrows pointing to heaven. Winter already crowned faraway crests with snow, a sign that Honor's Glory would soon be enveloped with the same. Widow's Peak rose above a blue-green lake surrounded by a meadow blanketed in late summer wildflowers. Mountain mint wafted on the breeze, bringing with it the hum of dragonflies and honeybees.

A cathedral-like hush lay over the land, as if the mountains themselves waited for God to speak this day. Awe and reverence humbled Sayra. No where else on earth had she ever felt so close to her Lord; no where else had she ever quite experienced the beauty of His immense power.

"It takes your breath away." Every word that came to mind seemed unworthy to describe the peace that enveloped her. As if the dawn itself filled her pores, Sayra felt a warmth begin at her toes and slowly embrace her. And in its wake, came strength—renewed purpose, hope, courage to believe again what once had seemed impossible.

Lily took the blanket Aud carried and spread it out over the ground. "Come, Aunt Sayra. Let's have church. I feel like the Lord will be sitting right beside me this morning, don't you?"

Aud's glacial blue eyes gleamed with pleasure. "I don't know of anyone who can come up here and not feel that way, Miss Lily. My guess is if you've got something laying heavy on your heart, this is the best place to let it go. He's sure to hear it this close."

Though their employer's words had been aimed at Lily, Sayra realized Aud's eyes were focused on her. Her first instinct was to look away, but the astute miner would know immediately she'd guessed right.

"Come on, Miss Sayra. I ain't been no angel, myself. No need to worry about me telling none of your regrets. I reckon if I'm lucky enough to get to greet the Lord personally one day, then the best I can figure on getting is a pair of clipped wings. You think I get these roughed-up knees from crawling around in the mine. . . ?"

Sayra's attention focused on the stains at Aud's knees. She had thought exactly that.

". . .Well, if you do, you're wrong. That's from bending my knees and asking forgiveness every single day when I fall short'a what He means for me to do with this here life. So don't you go frettin' that you might say something to the Lord that'll surprise me. I ain't your judge and salvation. He is. I got my own soul to spit polish."

A smile warmed Sayra's heart, lifting her lips into a broad grin. Without further hesitation, she joined the miner and her niece on the blanket and sank to her knees. With hands palmed together in reverence toward her Maker, she bowed her head and joined her companions in prayer.

The heavy load of troubles she'd carried on her back for weeks now fled as Sayra poured out her heart to God. She accepted the responsibility for her actions, asked Him for forgiveness, and thanked Him for His guiding grace in all she did. "Please Lord," she whispered reverently, "if it be Your will, lead me to where You would have us go. And if it be Your will, guide us to the man who will become Lily's helpmate so that she might experience the great power of love You've promised to us all."

"Aaaamen," Lily proclaimed loudly, "and do it soon, Lord. I'm nearly seventeen."

A chuckle erupted from Aud as one eye slid open just enough to give the pair a quick survey, then immediately closed again. "Oh and Lord, while You're alistening, teach my new cook and house cleaner a little perseverance. They ain't like us miners. . .they still gotta learn it ain't the gold you find that's the real treasure, but all that digging you gotta do to see if you're up to the search. That's the real blessing."

Sayra stood. Tiny needles of pain jabbed at her knees

and calves until finally feeling came back into her legs. "Goodness, I'm hungry!"

Aud and Lily turned and sat down on the blanket, resting their own knees. Aud motioned Sayra to join them, but she said she would stand awhile.

"You're hungry because you've cleansed your soul and handed over all your problems to the Lord," Aud informed her. "Now you've got to feed yourself a little faith."

A brow arched over one of Sayra's eyes. "Oh? How's that?"

"Why not write to your brother-in-law, Ulysses, and tell him the real reason you took Lily with you? Also, explain to him why you came here to Honor's Glory."

"I thought you weren't going to listen to my prayers?"

Aud shook her head, setting the cap's beaver tail to swishing back and forth like a furry pendulum. "I never said such. I did say I wouldn't be to judging ya."

Lily's eyes rounded, defense filling their blue-violet depths. "That's right, Aunt Sayra. She didn't."

Sayra sighed deeply. "All right, I suppose that's so. But I'm afraid to tell Ulysses. I know he'll come get her." It was the first time she'd spoken her fear aloud to her niece. "And I just can't let her go back until he's ready to spend more time with his family. He's too busy with his production quotas to worry about anything else."

A look of compassion filled Aud's face. "Since when did you earn the right to sit in judgment, Sayra? Only God knows the hour, remember, and that means the best hour for Ulysses to discover what's important to him."

The miner's words hit Sayra like an avalanche. She

stared at Lily, then her employer, and turned to the panorama that stretched as far as she could see. After a few moments of soul searching, she whispered, "You're right, Aud. I've tried to take life into my own hands and jerk it around like a puppet. But the strings I'm fighting are ties that will always be there. It was wrong to rush Lily away. I should have stayed. Perhaps if I'd been as patient with him as I expected him to be of Lily, Lily and I wouldn't be worrying where we're going to spend the winter. Maybe I will sit down and write him that I'm sorry for blaming him. Sorry that I hadn't given him a chance to change."

"You do that," Aud said and rose. "We best be getting on home now. Don't want to miss too much of my day of rest, either." As they began to fold the blanket, Aud reminded them, "I said the two of you could stay the winter with me, if you've a mind to. I meant it. Got used to the company, you know."

Sayra shook her head. "You only have enough supplies to hold out for one, Audrey, and we aren't going to let you do without just to make us think there's enough for all." She placed a hand upon Aud's arm and pressed gently. "You were kind to take us in when we really needed a place." Flinging the other arm wide, Sayra motioned toward the mountains in the distance. "It was good you brought us here. It's filled me with courage again. Courage and hope I'd thought I'd lost somewhere along the way. Now, I truly believe that somewhere out there is a home for Lily and me. I might even be looking at it now. Maybe Ulysses won't mind her staying with me, if I ask his forgiveness for taking her."

"Won't know 'til you try, will ya, gal?" Aud responded.

"Right again. Is that a habit you picked up from working the mines?" Sayra teased.

"No. Learned it the hard way. Got tired of being wrong all the time, so decided I'd try something new. Ain't never too late, you know. Sure can make the future look mighty bright where you're going."

A future for both of us, Sayra prayed silently, one that might lead her once again to Truman Taylor after she helped Lily find a safe, happy place in life.

"Wherever we're going," Lily announced solemnly, *"I hope it's easier to get to than here."*

❧

"Read the letter, Aunt Sayra." Lily couldn't stand still.

Sayra took the folded page and scanned the words quickly, deciding to hold back any news or discussion that might dampen her niece's enthusiasm about the correspondence from home. Her fingers trembled as she realized the anger or accusations she'd expected from Ulysses were not included in the reply to the letter she'd sent two weeks ago.

"Dear Sayra and Lily," she read aloud, clearing her throat of the emotion that had welled there.

> *"It is so good to hear from you. We
> learned from the fort commander at
> Julesberg that you had given up your job
> with the telegraph and headed north.
> Correspondence with your former
> employer, Truman Taylor, proved worri-
> some. He had intended to follow up on*

a search for the two of you, but something about pressing trouble with an officer at the fort kept him from pursuing it further.

"When he indicated that none of the telegraph stations knew of your current whereabouts, I started to take the first stage to Julesberg, but Bess insisted that I didn't. Good thing I didn't, or I would have missed your letter. And if the truth won't anger you further, I'm having trouble with the gin and need to stay nearby until I can get that resolved. Perhaps then, I and the family can come see this Colorado my Lily speaks so highly of.

"I assumed, and rightly so, it seems, that you might have been low on funds and had taken up residence in a less comely township.

"Please express my sincerest gratitude to Miss Williams for allowing you the use of her home. I'm most curious about a residence called, It'll Do. In the event Miss Williams's hospitality has overextended her winter savings, I've sent along a tidy sum to be given to her in repayment for your stay.

"The remainder is a small payment to you, Sayra. Your parents owned the land long before us; it's only right that you should receive some part of the profit each season. I'm truly regretful about

*the reason you and Lily left and have
sought penance with the Lord. I hope
you accept this small sum and my
sincerest thanks that you had the sense
of heart and presence of mind to do what
was best for our daughter.*

   *"Though it should not be difficult for
me to say this, I still find it so. I'm
sorry, Sayra, for the wrong I committed
against my daughter. Lily, if you're
reading this yourself, I'm sorry I didn't
give you the one thing I could, the only
thing you ever asked of me, sweet child.
Time. Can you forgive me?"*

"We can, can't we, Aunt Sayra? He was terribly busy
and awfully tired. He didn't mean to pay me no attention."

Sayra glanced up to see eyes filled with compassion
staring at her, waiting for permission. "I can't make
that decision for you. If you forgive your father, that's
all that matters."

"But do you?"

"Yes, I do," Sayra replied honestly. She knew she
had ever since Aud had taken them up on Widow's Peak
that first time. She'd even pardoned herself for running away from the real reason they'd left. The relief
that filled her now made Sayra realize she'd been
waiting for Ulysses to absolve her, hoping he would
understand that she'd acted purely out of love for Lily.

"Will you be going home?" Aud appeared at the
door of the mine shack, her hands filled with a sack of
flour she'd bought back from town. She'd spent all

morning in Honor's Glory, bringing back supplies and the letter from Ulysses.

Sayra looked at Lily. "It's a decision we both must make. What do you prefer, Blossom, Port Hudson or somewhere in Colorado?"

"Papa said he's still having to work hard, didn't he?" Lily took the letter Sayra offered and scanned through it. "Yeah, right here it says so. And he did say he wanted to see my Colorado. If I go home, he wouldn't get to see it." Lily's expression filled with determination. "Colorado is pretty and makes me feel happy. It doesn't have that ugly old order, either. I don't like watching all those soldiers make fun of people. If I go back, I might kick one in the ankle again."

"Then it's settled. We stay in Colorado." Sayra held the sum that had been sent to her. "But this won't last forever. I must find employment. . .and soon."

Aud set the sack over in the corner and took a chair opposite Lily and Sayra at the table. "Well, then I guess I oughta go ahead and tell you about the telegrapher's job that got posted on the livery tent. Stationmaster said the regular brass pounder left for Wyoming. You might still have a chance to hire on, if you're interested."

A telegrapher's job? Sayra felt as if her prayers had been answered. Visions of a telegrapher's tent much like the one Jubilee and Molly must man at Badger Springs came to mind. "A telegraph. Here in Honor's Glory?" she asked expectantly.

The miner studied her fingernails for a moment, her voice gruff. "No. It's up Georgetown way. Near Denver."

"But that means we'd have to leave you," Lily reasoned aloud. "I don't know if I want to leave you, Aud."

Aud patted Lily's hand. "And I'm going to miss you, too, Miss Lily. I ain't never had such a best friend in all my life." She sniffled and wiped her buckskinned sleeve across her nose. "Guess I gotta cold. Always do that when I visit town too much."

Though she attempted to hide the emotions riffling through her, Sayra knew that the hard-as-a-tack lady miner was on the verge of tears.

"Just 'cause you hightail it to Georgetown don't mean I cain't come and visit ya. Fact is, I might feel it an obligation sometime to see if you two are setting your lives to right, just like you promised the Lord up on my mountain. Besides, like Sayra said that day. . .I ain't got enough supplies and funds to feed the lot of us this whole winter. You two would be better off up in Georgetown. At least there you'll have decent hotels and boarding houses. Something more than canvas over your heads and dirt floors to warm your feet. Sayra, you go on and get that telegrapher's job, and Miss Lily, you do what you can to find that husband who's going to love all the special things you are. You won't find 'im sitting up here on this mountain cooking for an old gal like me."

"If I do, will you come to my wedding?" Lily's tone revealed how much the miner's answer meant to her.

A grin stretched across Aud's face as she attempted to liven the mood. "Why, I'll do better than that. I'll come dressed in bloomers and frills."

Lily held out her hand and waited for Aud to lock palms. "That's a deal, partner," she proclaimed, pumping the miner's palm vigorously. "It'd be worth it to find a husband just to get to see you in a dress!"

Aud issued her own challenge. "Tell you what, Miss Lily. You help your aunt get that job, then go about

marrying up a man—the right kind of man, mind you—
and I'll work on finding me that piece of frills and the
gold to buy it with."

Sayra laughed. "Now that our futures are set, when
do you plan to tell Turk how much you care for him?"

"Posh!" Aud exclaimed, rising to fetch herself a cup
of coffee warming on the stove. "Me and Turk?
That'll happen when the desert freezes over."

"Practice what you preach, dear friend." Sayra accepted a cup of coffee from Aud. "You tell us to get on
with our lives and let someone love us for all that we
are. Why don't you tell Turk the truth?"

"'Cause he'll rant and rave 'til the snow dries up,
that's why."

"Then he'll realize that all these years he loved you
more than as a friend. You had me confess to Ulysses
and ask his forgiveness; why can't you do the same to
Turk?"

New purpose straightened Aud's shoulders as she set
her coffee cup down on the table. "You know I might
just at that. . .after I've carried you gals into Honor to
catch the next stage. And *after* you promise me, Sayra,
that you'll do the same thing to that Truman Taylor
fellow you pine about in your sleep." She raised a hand
to ward off Sayra's denial. "Don't try to fool an old
pretender like me. Dreams are like the past, the present,
and the future all rolled up into one. I'd say you're
staking a lot of your future on that fella, whether you
want to admit it or not. So I'll tell my Turk the truth, if
you'll make a point of seeing that Taylor fella again."

"All right," Sayra agreed as she took a sip of coffee.
Though any chance of meeting up with Truman Taylor again seemed as elusive as the vapors rising from
the cup's brim.

eleven

"I've never seen you like this, Tru. Are you sure you're going to hire this woman—or will you string her up?"

"Hire her." Truman let the curtain fall back into place and turned from the sight of the wagon that had just pulled in at the stationhouse. He didn't recognize the fair-haired fellow in the bear cape, but there was no mistaking Lily Van Buren's sweet laughter as she lowered herself down from the wagon, or the alluring beauty of her aunt as Sayra joined the travelers on the sidewalk.

Though Tru's gaze swept across the orderly telegraph office, noting that his adoptive brother was as efficient with his deciphering and filing as he was with bronc busting, the image of Sayra refused to fade. The click-click-clicks of the telegraph echoed in his mind as he recalled the lonely week in which he had found a true friend—a week of his life that now seemed long ago. Filled with laughter and shared stories, the game of Taps he and Sayra played had given him a sense of peace. Yet more importantly. . .it revived old dreams and stirred hopes he thought long buried.

"She's too good at what she does to let her out of our hands again," Truman spoke his thoughts aloud as he stared at the telegraph keys and could almost see them move. No matter what line she manned, he would never again hear the code tapped in over the wire without recognizing her own particular rhythm.

The sensation that he was being watched jerked his attention from the machine. Tru realized Shago was staring at him. "Why are you grinning like that?"

"No reason." Shago's cheeks dimpled on both sides as his grin became an all-out smile. "Except I think maybe I want to know what really went on between you two in Julesberg."

Truman ignored his brother's probing gaze. "You've got too much time on your hands, Shago. Like I said, we only saw each other once."

An honest statement if ever there was one, but deep within his heart, Truman felt he knew Sayra Martin better than he'd ever known Ginny. The sad part of it all was he couldn't remember a single time he and his wife had enjoyed talking to one another. He'd been too busy trying to carve out a life for them here in the West, while she'd been too consumed with plotting ways to head East. Perhaps if he'd spent more time being companion to her than provider. . . The guilt of wondering how he could have made things better for her never left him. The pain of recalling their last conversation before she died still haunted his sleepless nights. He'd believed in "for better and for worse," as well as "'til death do us part," but Ginny wanted out of their marriage almost before the wedding bouquet wilted.

"You think I want to spend my life in tent cities and clapboard shacks?" The shrill pitch of her voice rose like the screech of a chicken hawk.

As memory came rushing in, Tru forced himself to focus on anything but Shago's face. The boy read his moods and expressions too easily. No need to worry him. Yet the image of the last night with Ginny refused to fade.

"You think I really *loved* you?" Ginny's eyes had narrowed in contempt. "You were merely my ticket out of Richmond."

Her laughter, the wild look in her eyes as she had flung open the door and openly flaunted the lover waiting for her in the surrey had been too much to bear. Truman had chosen to turn from the sight that storm-filled night. He had accepted that the only way he could make her happy was to let her go, and it proved to be one of the most difficult choices he'd ever made.

A choice that ultimately put her in her grave. He should have demanded she stay and honor her vows. He should have said or done something that could have made things different. But *what?*

That singular question had festered for years, infecting his heart with a mistrust layered so deep no one could get close enough to heal his heart's loneliness . . .until Sayra came into his life. Though he'd jokingly said it was only a game of Taps, in truth they'd shared his life and laughter, the tears and failures of his youth, the heartache of loving and having lost. Sayra had somehow broken through that protective barrier. Like the wall of Jericho, the stone he'd spent so many years erecting suddenly crumbled in the wake of her sweet caring. Perhaps that's why his anger with her now seemed almost more than he could endure. Truman had shared his secrets with Sayra Martin and, like Ginny, she'd chosen to run with them. . .after he'd trusted her to stay.

Grabbing his brother's hat down from the rack, Tru

tossed it onto the desk. "Why don't you saunter on over there to Brewster's Place and get yourself a haircut? Morrell will be mistaking you for that upstart George Armstrong Custer, if it gets any longer."

Shago rubbed the point of his first grown beard and moustache as his attention focused on a piece of rawhide that lay near a stack of telegrams. With deft fingers, he tied back the tawny-colored hair that now fell in waves to mid-shoulder. "See? Easily repaired," he teased, picking up his hat and nestling it over his head, "and saved me a hard-earned nickel."

The seventeen-year-old stood and moved away from the desk. "Now don't go snarling your face up like that, Tru. I remember a whole winter you didn't cut your hair." Amusement slitted Shago's gray eyes. "Near as I remember it, Ol' Gus Neddlebaum almost mistook you for a longhorn sheep that winter. Might've sheared you himself if I hadn't convinced him you and your horse took up lame and you were forced to spend the night in his corral."

Truman laughed. "I heard his missus finally persuaded him to get some spectacles. Said she was tired of him making one of himself."

"Speaking of spectacles. I've never seen you make yourself one over a woman before. I'd like to get a look at this lady telegrapher." Shago strode over to the window and peeked out the curtain. His neck craned first one way then another as if he couldn't quite focus on a particular sight. Finally, he turned back toward Truman.

"Something's set a burr under your saddle to get me out of the office in such an all-fired hurry. Now where is she? That is the wagon Miss Martin arrived in over at the stationhouse, isn't it?"

"She got off it."

"Ooohh, aren't we a little ruffled?" Shago opened the office door and let it stand ajar. "So, I take it she wasn't alone?"

"Her niece travels with her."

"That wasn't a niece kind of snarl you just gave me. If I were a betting man, I'd guess that was a another-man-rode-in-with-your-woman kind of sneer."

Truman grabbed a stack of telegrams and glanced through them. "What she does away from this office is no concern of mine. Now, you go on and get your business taken care of. I'll want you here so I can introduce you to her and have you show her why we run this office a bit different than the others."

Shago's eyes widened. "Ohh, don't fret about that, brother mine. I wouldn't miss this introduction for the world. No way I'm gonna miss meeting the lady who was able to rouse Truman Taylor out of his self-pity. No sir, not me."

"Get on out of here, before we have one of our disagreements," Tru warned, angered at being accused of feeling sorry for himself, yet twice as irritated because he knew Shago was right. "I'd rather the office still be in some kind of order when the new telegrapher arrives."

The younger man gave a sweeping bow, then rested both palms over his heart. "By all means, Ol' Great Supernumerary. Would but that you ask your simple servant to do more, and I would humbly—"

"Save the Shakespeare, Shago. I'm not in the mood for dramatics."

A telegram sailed through the air, landing far short

of its intended target. Shago laughed and backed out of the door, putting his hands up in mock surrender. "Thou dost woundeth my soul, big brotheroth. Alas, now I must face the day with great sorrow in my heart and—"

"Scat!" Truman half roared, half chuckled, unable to withstand the melodramatic expression darting across Shago's face.

"Begonst, brother," Shago corrected, continuing to back farther into the street. "A word far more appropriate and less pesty."

"Look out!" Truman yelled, rushing forward to stop the collision. "Behind you!"

"Watch where you're going!" a voice sounded from behind Shago.

The seventeen-year-old turned, stumbled, and attempted to keep his footing but failed. Momentum drove him downward into the laps of the two women now sprawled beneath him.

Truman raced to his side, grabbed one of his brother's arms, and helped him get to his knees. "Sorry about this, ladies." A quick inspection revealed Shago was not hurt but attempting to regain the air that seemed to have escaped him on impact. "My brother's usually a bit more agile than this."

"I'm not sure it was such a pleasure to meet you, Mr. Taylor." Lily held out her hand, and Shago instantly reached out to help her up. He gripped too hard, and her glove began to slide, then flew off. She slid backward, landing with a thud in the dirt once again. "I'll say one thing for your greetings; they sure pack a wallop."

"I'm terribly sorry, miss. Are you hurt? Can I help?" When she started moving away from him in the sand,

Shago quickly straightened and took a couple of steps backward. "Don't scoot no further. I'll quit trying to help, miss. My name's Shago. Shago Jones. Tru and I don't share the same last names."

"Nor good balance either," Lily noted, rubbing her backside.

Shago's skin turned redder than a ripened beet.

Sayra Martin rose and began dusting the folds of her skirt. She tried to speak, but her words came out flustered. Truman was suddenly aware that she was not angry at having been knocked down. Some other emotion made speech difficult for her.

"W-What are you doing here?" she finally asked, her violet eyes rounded in surprise. "I thought you were still in Julesberg."

"This is her?" Shago took her hand and shook it vigorously. Frank admiration filled his eyes. "No wonder you've been all out of sorts lately, brother. I would have too if she'd walked out of my—"

"Why don't you see if Miss Lily needs help getting to the office, Shago," Truman reminded sternly, ending his brother's gawking before he made a fool of both of them. "Miss Martin and I have a few things to discuss alone."

"No, thank you." Lily's chin tilted upward. "I can get there all by myself. And in one piece."

A whooshing sound filled the air. All eyes focused on Shago as his lips created the strange sound while his hands fisted over his heart and the young telegrapher pretended an arrow had pierced him there. "Alas, my lady, but you have wounded me to the core. I fear I cannot drawest another breath until ye forgivest my foolhardiness."

Lily's own fists knotted against her hips. "Does all that fancy talk mean you're going to watch where you're going from now on?"

Shago bowed low, waving one hand in front of him as if conceding to royalty. "Should it so please the lady."

"Well, please yourself, mister. Just remember that if you don't watch where you're going, you certainly can't get there." In a huff, she started toward the building marked Western Union Telegraph.

Before hurrying after her, Shago shared a glance with Tru. "A sage, she is. . .after my own heart." Hearing the slam of the office door inspired challenge in his eyes, ". . .and a shrew!"

Truman watched his brother's stride quicken and knew beyond a doubt that Shago's days would be spent getting to know the delightful Miss Lily. The thought pleased him and hope stirred within. Though Lily was a month or two younger than his adoptive brother, Tru had no doubt that if the minx was anything like her aunt, she would teach Shago a lesson or two about enjoying life to the fullest.

"They would make a lovely couple," Sayra commented as if she could read his mind.

"Who. . .them?" Truman pretended his thoughts were elsewhere. "I suppose so."

"She's a perfectly fine match for someone."

The anger in her voice surprised Truman. He hadn't meant to offend Sayra and certainly meant nothing derogatory about Lily. "Lily will make some man a wonderful wife. I know I only met her once, but from what you told me about her that night, I feel like I already know her."

"I'm sorry, Truman," Sayra said sincerely. "Some people treat Lily differently, and my first impulse is to defend her. I shouldn't have assumed you were the same."

"It seems to me from what I saw, Lily's perfectly capable of standing up for herself," he chuckled. "I guess that's a bad choice of words, considering Shago knocked her down twice."

Sayra joined in his laughter, enjoying the release of tension it offered. "You're right, you know. She always manages to hold her own. I don't give Lily her due. I must stop that. Thanks for reminding me."

The time for reminding had come, and Truman almost wished he could let it go. But he couldn't. The hurt was too deep. Keeping silent had driven Ginny away. Maybe demanding an explanation wouldn't bring him and Sayra Martin any closer, but at least he would be able to understand why she'd left Julesberg and the beginning of what he hoped might become more than friendship.

There seemed no way to ease into the subject. "You left Julesberg."

She looked away. "I'll pay back the advance. You can count on it."

His eyes raised to the sun, closing while he garnered the strength to hear the truth. "You know I'm not talking about the money. I have no doubt you'll pay the company back, Sayra. Your honor is not in question here. . .is it?" There, he'd asked her outright.

Concern welled in him like a great wind, twisting and turning, gathering momentum as the seconds ticked by and she did not speak.

"Did you leave because of Parker Quinton?" Truman

demanded, detesting that he could not let his curiosity rest. He needed to know that the major had not compromised her in any fashion.

"No."

After another eternal silence, Truman became exasperated. "Just no? A simple no? Do you have any idea how much I wondered and worried why you left? Asked myself a million questions as to why you would leave without—"

Her eyes widened into sympathetic pools of regret. "Without telling you," she finished for him. Her hand shot out and touched his arm as if to reassure him. "Oh, Truman, I never once considered that you would take my leaving personally. Never once. I have reasons that I'd rather not go into now, but it wasn't because of the major and certainly had nothing to do with you."

"Yet you can't tell me why?"

"It's none of your concern." Her hand slid softly to her side.

Hurt, deep and swift, pierced his heart, making it feel as if it would jump out of his chest. As he had done in all the years since Ginny's death, he mortared another brick in the wall that encased his battered heart and turned away from her. "You're right, Miss Martin. Nothing you do is any of my business. . .except that you show up for work at seven o'clock tomorrow morning ready to do your job. You owe the Western Union money, and I intend to see that you earn it. After you come in and discuss your duties with Shago, I'll bid you and your niece a pleasant good day."

Long after she'd gone and the sun had set behind the Rockies, Truman Taylor decided this night was shaping up to be one of the longest of his entire life.

twelve

Georgetown proved to be an active settlement, providing a stop-off point between Denver and routes heading west into California and Oregon. Though gaming saloons were in abundance, the citizenry had wisely erected churches and schools to entice settlers who knew the value of such establishments. Few settlements along the Continental Divide shared such a law-abiding reputation, making Georgetown one of the more respectable Colorado communities. Sayra took to her job like a bee to its honeycomb. Though the office was in far better order than the one at Julesberg, business flowed through the Georgetown telegraph station like a rain-gorged river. She moved through the ensuing days, deliberately pushing herself to work harder and faster so she would not have time to mourn what might have been between her and Truman.

Sleep eluded her. Each night the memory of her words haunted Sayra. *It's none of your concern.* Cruel words, perhaps, but the truth. She was his employee. She owed his company money. They'd merely shared a game of Taps, hadn't they?

As she had every night since arriving in the settlement, Sayra rose, dressed, and left the boarding-house room where she and Lily now resided. It didn't have the same feeling of "home" Mrs. Kou's house offered, but its gingerbread architecture and Victorian furnishings were pleasantly appealing and clean. The landlady was likeable enough, and she allowed Lily to cook, when the girl took the notion.

A hazy glow rimmed the moon, warning that bad weather would be setting in tomorrow or the day after. Glad she had grabbed her heavy serge coat, Sayra pushed her chin deeper into its warmth so that her lips and ears were not exposed to the cold.

Down the street an amber glow emanated from several of the saloons. Raucous laughter and tinny music carried on the breeze. The Western Union had been wise enough to build its office on the north end of town, near one of the churches and the school—a decision she'd since learned was made for precaution rather than from simple morality. If attacked, the company knew the townsfolk would first defend the school and church, leaving the red-light district to its own fate. Whatever their reason, Sayra appreciated the outcome, for she felt safe taking a midnight stroll along the boardwalk in front of the storefronts. The sheriff's deputy made rounds every two hours, keeping careful watch on the town's best assets.

Once again her steps led her to the telegraph office where she might prove helpful to Shago. The workhorse ethic remained as much a part of her as breathing, and to be idle seemed time unnecessarily lost. Besides, there was always enough work to keep two people busy.

Surprisingly, tonight she found her co-worker alone and taking a coffee break. "I do believe this is the first time I've ever seen the office empty," she remarked, hanging the serge coat on the hook behind the door.

The metal sides of the stove standing beside the desk glowed red, emitting a comforting warmth that easily devoured the chill she'd momentarily allowed into the room.

"And I believe you haven't slept more than a few hours any night this week." Shago looked up from his mug. "Seems you just have time to get some supper, visit a while with Miss Lily, then come trotting over here like you don't have anything better to do. You're going to wear yourself out, Sayra."

"Might as well work; I can't rest."

"You could if you two would quit torturing each other and start talking."

There was no denying which "two" he meant. Self-consciously, Sayra pressed a hand to the back of her hair to make certain the hairpins still held her curls inside the chignon at the nape of her neck.

"Come sit for a while, at least." Shago waved her toward the chair opposite his desk. "I didn't mean to make you feel uncomfortable. Want to talk about it? I could use a bit of conversation that doesn't dot, dash, or hum at me."

Sayra laughed, accepting the cup of coffee he poured and seating herself across from him. "I know how you feel. Is Georgetown always so busy? Sometimes I think we must be the communication's depot of the West."

Shago set the coffeepot back on the stove and sat down. "Every one west is eager for news about their families back East. The cavalry wants updates on the Indian campaigns, and the East demands information about the latest gold and silver strikes. But the success of this office isn't what's really on your mind, Sayra."

"Does it show that much?" Sayra's eyes focused on her hands as they gripped the mug. Sayra studied the brim as if it contained answers to what troubled her.

"Look at me."

His demand lifted her gaze, instantly drawing it to the concern written in his face.

"You two have been dodging each other like you both have the pox. Yet I've seen you when Tru's here. You watch every move he makes when he's not looking. And Tru? That man's working himself from dusk to dawn, just so he can saunter into the office any time of the day to see what you're up to."

"He just wants to make certain I stay and pay the company back the money he loaned me." *And to make sure I don't run away* were the words on the tip of her tongue, but she didn't add them.

"You gave him your word. That's good enough for Tru."

Sayra blushed. "I'm afraid I did that once before and disappointed him."

"He doesn't hold a grudge against other people," Shago reassured her, "just himself. No ma'am, he's spending his days as close to town and you as possible. Makes it difficult to troubleshoot the line. . .having to work by lantern light."

"Do you mean he's not sleeping at all?"

"If he is, it sure ain't in his own bed."

Considering the alternative disturbed her. Sayra sensed her co-worker's regard and didn't want him to know where his statement led her thoughts. "Perhaps he's like me. . .restless."

Shago sipped his coffee. "Maybe. All I know is I gotta

do something about it. He's been as touchy as an old bear lately and getting even grumpier. If I can't get that brother of mine to hibernate for a few hours, things around here are fixing to get meaner than a hound dog looking for his best bone."

"Surely you can talk some sense into him. I can't imagine you not being able to convince Truman to do just about anything you want him to; he thinks so highly of you."

Affection lifted Shago's lips. "Yeah, I'm pretty lucky to call him family. But I'm not the one who needs to convince him. You've gotta put his mind at ease. . .or better yet, his heart."

"His heart?"

Shago reached out and placed his hand over hers to stop the nervous tapping her fingers made against the cup. "Yeah, his heart. If you don't know by now that Big Brother is wearing his heart on his sleeve where you're concerned, then you're nowhere near as smart a lady as I'm giving you credit for. You do love him, don't you?"

"Love?" The word spread through Sayra like sunshine warming new seed.

Love, like what Mother and Father shared? The seed took root and grew.

Love, like that God meant between man and woman? Hope filled her, blossoming into a commitment that made her soul sing with gladness.

But the voice of reason whispered she was not some child who could allow herself the luxury of love at first sight. She couldn't cast these seeds of love onto barren ground. Her faith wavered as she spoke the fear aloud, "He doesn't care for *me*, does he?"

"That's not what I asked. I want to know if you love him."

"Love? Perhaps that's a bit premature. I haven't known him long."

"But you're at least interested in finding out?"

"I suppose. What does that have to do with anything?"

Shago stood and leaned over the desk, exasperation making his fists ball against the tabletop. "It has to do with *everything*, don't you see? Truman doesn't think he deserves a woman like you. He keeps on blaming himself for Ginny's death, thinking if he'd have done this or that, things would be different. He can't accept that she would have left no matter how hard he tried to make her stay."

She found it difficult to meet Shago eye-to-eye, but forced herself not to look away. "I left him, too, without saying good-bye. . .without telling him why."

"You're sorry you did that, aren't you?"

"Of course, I am."

"Then that's the difference." Shago straightened. "Ginny never was. She never loved him. You might. He'll forgive you, Sayra, but he needs you to help him learn to forgive himself."

Something sparked inside Sayra, and she sensed her past now lay in ashes. Excitement filled her, whispering that there could be a new beginning for her and Truman. A beginning filled with honesty and trust.

"Perhaps tomorrow, when he comes into the office, he and I can have a long talk." A deep sigh escaped her, freeing her of long-held troubles that no longer seemed insurmountable.

Shago thumbed through the telegrams and stopped when he found a particular one. "Here, read this. Tru left it for you and said not to let you work tomorrow."

Sayra quickly scanned the note. He'd given her the day off, telling her he assumed she would want to go to church services. He'd even invited her to sit in the Taylor pew. "Will you be going?" she asked. "I wouldn't want you to miss the service because of me."

"I can see there are still some things you don't know about Tru." Shago grabbed a jar containing a small portion of earth and a tiny seed. "Recognize this?"

At first Sayra didn't, then she realized she'd seen it on the Julesberg desk, as well. "It belongs to Truman, doesn't it?"

Shago nodded. "It goes wherever Tru goes. It's sort of a reminder, I guess you'd say. In the Bible, there's the old saying that if you but have the faith of a mustard seed, you can move mountains."

"I remember."

"Well, Tru says you reminded him how just a seed of faith has gotten him through some pretty rough times in the past. How a man shouldn't just say he has religion, but live it. Living it means going to services if he's in town. Or if he happens to be away from home, then he should find a place to bend his knees there, too."

"I know someone else who does that," Sayra interjected, "my friend, Aud. You know, you met he—him when he brought us to Georgetown."

"Yeah, Lily's man friend. Too old for her, if you ask me, but he does have good taste in women." The frown eased from Shago's forehead. "Anyway, you can bet Tru reminded me the Taylor pew had been empty long enough now and there better be only one reason I'd miss being there tomorrow morning. . .if I was injured or ill."

Good manners kept her from asking, and an unspoken code of the West demanded that she mind her own business, but Sayra wondered whether Shago resented having a different last name than Truman. "I suppose there isn't a Jones pew in the congregation?"

"Oh, there's always a Jones pew in any congregation; just not one particularly belonging to me and my kin. Most folks around here know why." Her curiosity seemed not to bother him at all. Shago's eyes focused beyond Sayra, as if recalling some long ago happening. "Not much to tell but that my parents decided to head west to the Colorado gold fields and strike it rich. All they got for their troubles was a deadly case of diptheria. The wagon train we were traveling with made us leave the circle and follow at a distance. But Ma took real sick and Pa decided we best camp. My sister, Mattie Pearl, was buried two days later. I was burning up with fever and don't remember much more than hearing Papa's hoarse whispers, begging my ma not to die."

Tears burned in Shago's eyes, making him blink several times. "When I woke up, I was staring at Tru, a total stranger. Though he was sweating like the sun was scorching, it was during the first snow of winter when he found me. He'd buried my family and set everything ablaze. He put his own life in danger to sling me across his horse and carry me into South Pass. When I was well enough to travel, he took me home with him and has taken care of me ever since. That was five years ago. Tru's was the only home I knew. So, there's no way on this earth I'd miss sitting alongside him in the Taylor pew, Miss Sayra. That is, until I scooted over for his bride."

Loud scrapes on the sidewalk outside the door warned they had a customer even before the door opened, sending a blast of cold through the room. Sayra gripped her arms, warding off the chill, and turned to greet the late-night visitor.

The familiar sight of Truman Taylor's broad shoulders, dark hair, and powerful physique swept the chill instantly away. When she met his gaze, his eyes grew darker. . .or perhaps it was merely the burst of wind coming through the opened door that caused the lanterns' flames to flicker and the emerald hue of his eyes to deepen.

She tried to look away, but his close scrutiny held her transfixed. Sayra yearned to go to him, take the coat from his back, offer coffee to warm him, and gently soothe away the dark circles beneath his eyes.

Longing swept through Sayra—a need so deep it nearly took her breath away. She wanted to tell Truman she thought she loved him, wanted to care for him and provide his every comfort. Yet words would not suffice. She had to show him—prove to him and herself that she would never again break her word, run away, or hold back the truth.

"I hoped you'd be here." His voice was deep, masculine, compelling. "Didn't want to wake up everybody at the boarding house, being as late as it is."

Turbulent emotions whirled through Sayra. An intangible bond connected them, yet kept them at a distance from one another for a reason she could not comprehend. Perhaps with patience she would know. Perhaps in God's time, she would understand. "You needed me?"

Truman took off his hat, setting a dark curl free to dangle across his brow. "Would you do me the honor of accompanying me to church in the morning?"

Shago shouted a loud hurrah. When two pair of eyes focused on him, his lips lifted into a half-grin. "Okay, so my vote is that she says yes." His tone became more plea than demand, "Say yes, Sayra, and get me out of this awkward moment."

"Yes, Truman. I'd love to go with you. On one condition. . ." Sayra laughed as joy filled her heart and a prayer silently lifted into the great beyond. *Thank You, thank You, thank You, Lord, for bringing such wonderful men into my life. For showing me how to forgive myself. For being patient with me when I needed to learn of patience myself. Now teach me a way to help Truman forgive himself and find peace within.* "Promise to go straight to your room and get some sleep until thirty minutes before services begin."

For the first time since entering, Truman smiled. The sight nearly made Sayra's heart skip its rhythm, dazzling her with the rugged handsomeness of his features when eased of tension and exhaustion.

"Tell you what," Truman bargained, "I'll get some rest, if you'll ask Miss Lily to accompany Shago to church. It'll look mighty good having the Taylor pew full again."

Shago groaned. "You sure you don't need someone to man the office in the morning?"

"I told you we were closing for church, and I mean shut down."

"Don't you like my niece?" Surprise and a measure of defense rose in Sayra. She'd thought the pair had gotten along fairly well. ...except for the day Lily deliberately spilled ink on Shago's work after a long session of his teasing her. And she supposed the incident this morning when Lily slammed the office door in his face and said the wind had blown it shut, might be construed as disliking one another. Perhaps they weren't getting along as famously as she'd hoped.

"Like her?" Shago grimaced. "Ohhh, there's a lot to like about Lily." He rubbed his nose that still smarted from his last encounter with her. "If a fellow has a mind to court a porcupine."

"You can take that as a compliment, Sayra." Truman grabbed her serge coat from the rack and held it open for her. "Shago loves a challenge, and I think he realizes he's finally met his match."

"Haven't we all?" Sayra quipped innocently as she linked her arm through his and accepted his unspoken offer to escort her home.

thirteen

If there was mercy in heaven, Sayra hoped she would not be judged for the direction of her thoughts while in the Lord's house. Dressed in a black suit, white shirt, and string tie, Truman was the most handsome man she had ever had the privilege of meeting. Her heart soared with pride as he escorted her down the aisle that divided the large twenty-pew church. When she saw women turn and eye her employer with frank admiration, Sayra wondered how many of them, like herself, were attracted to more than the man's quality of character.

A murmur rippled across the congregation as she took a seat beside him. She felt eyes focused on her back, heard the volume of speculation increase when Lily sat alongside Shago as well. Sayra settled her gaze on the preacher, who stood behind the pulpit. Perhaps his sermon would be one that would lift all of them beyond their current curiosity and allow them to find not only peace, but inspiration in their faith.

Lily leaned past Shago. "Pssst! Aunt Sayra. Why are all these people looking at us so strange?"

Though her niece's words were meant to be hushed, Lily's voice carried amazingly far. Sayra smiled apologetically at several faces that turned around. "We're new. They're just curious."

A full-figured woman sitting in front of them turned,

causing the silver plume on her bonnet to brush the man's face sitting next to her. He sneezed. Shago said something that sounded like "ostrich." Lily giggled. Sayra blushed, and Truman offered the man a handkerchief.

"Thank you, Mr. Taylor." The woman lightly dabbed her own lace hankie at her nose. "I've told Henry to carry one, but he won't." She offered Sayra an expression that hinted her patience was being tested. "But you don't know how husbands are, I assure you." She said the word *husband* as if it were the most trying tribulation known to womankind. "I'm Loretta Osterman, my dear, and I can tell you the good people of Georgetown are more than merely 'curious' about you. I'm sure everyone wants to know how you managed to get two of the most eligible bachelors this side of the Continental Divide to escort you to service. Others here have tried and failed, I assure you."

Sayra didn't want the woman thinking either she or Lily had designs on Truman and Shago, since both brothers were simply doing a Christian kindness by sharing their pew. "I work for Mr. Taylor, ma'am. He and Shago were nice enough to ask my niece and I to sit with them this morning."

Shago cleared his throat, and Sayra heard the word "forced" in his pretended cough.

"Ouww!" the cough became an exclaimation of pain. The seventeen-year-old rubbed his side where Lily had elbowed him in the ribs.

Lily glared at her reluctant escort. "I don't want to be here with you any more than you do with me."

Loretta Osterman sighed. "A pity. I'd hoped the

Taylor pew would be brimming with new *attending* family members soon. Still, why don't you and the young lady come to supper one night this week? We can get to know—"

"Let us all stand and sing from page twenty-seven of your hymnals." The preacher waited until all rose.

"I'd love to," Sayra leaned forward and whispered quickly. In her search for a hymnal, she came up empty-handed. There were only two at this end of the pew, and Lily had grabbed one, Truman the other.

He thumbed it to the proper page and held it open in front of Sayra. Feeling a bit shy, she hesitated before finally moving closer so she could read the words. Their shoulders touched. As the first strains of the hymn echoed throughout the church, her eyes focused on Truman's strong face, noting the dark lashes that forested his emerald eyes. His own gaze was not focused on the words but rather looked beyond the preacher to the large cross centered on the wall beyond the pulpit.

The fact that he still knew the song by heart endeared Tru to her. That he sang directly to his Lord strangely comforted her. Sayra joined him in song, blending her alto to his baritone. When Truman hit an occasional wrong note, he simply looked at her, winked, and continued singing as if he were a virtuoso. The self-confidence it took to ignore what other people might feel about his less-than-perfect vocalizing increased the amount of respect she held for him.

Shago shared no such need for improvement. Never had Sayra heard such a voice in all her life. He transformed from a slight bearded youth who spouted Shakespeare to a man whose resonate tenor could make the angels weep in awe. That same wonder radiated on her niece's face, making Lily move closer to blend her own sweet soprano with his voice.

Sayra's soul quickened, sending a rush of knowing pebbling atop her skin. Just as she'd felt that morning on Widow's Peak when she experienced God's handiwork carved in mountain faces and winnowing in the meadow, she knew she was hearing Him now in voices gifted by divine will.

When the song ended, Lily expressed her admiration, "No boy who can sing like that is all worthless."

A chuckle escaped Truman as his hand rose immediately to wipe the grin from his mouth. He leaned closer, unable to hide his amusement. "I think that was a compliment, brother."

"That's good to know. But remind me never to ask her to be a witness of my character, should I ever need one." Shago took the hymnal Lily offered and placed it back where it belonged.

All the whispering caused a frown to wrinkle across the preacher's forehead. "Brothers and sisters," his voice boomed authoritatively, "I ask that you pay close heed to the message our Lord has laid upon my heart this morning. Today's sermon comes first from the book of John 1:9. 'If we confess our sins, He is faithful and just to forgive us our sins.' Now turn to Isaiah 43:25."

After a shuffling of pages rustled through the sanctuary, he read the verse, "'I, even I, am he that blotteth out thy transgressions.'" The preacher looked out into his congregation. "I ask you, is there one among you without a sin—a sin you've believed far too long God would never forgive? He says but to confess, and He will erase all transgressions."

Though the minister's gaze focused on the whole crowd, Sayra felt as if he were staring directly at her. Her eyes closed while she thanked the Lord for the choice of sermon. Was Tru listening? Did he hear what the clergyman reminded them of? That all he had to do was truly want forgiveness, ask for it, then God, in His grace, would wipe the slate clean forever.

Her soul needed baring. How could she help him if she didn't confess her own shortcomings, not only to God but to Truman himself? She continued to listen to the sermon, silently pouring out her heart to her Maker.

Tears trickled down Sayra's cheeks unashamedly as her prayers intensifed and she sensed that she was being heard. . .and that her life could somehow be brand new again. All the bad choices, mistaken good intentions, running away were forever erased from the slate that tallied her hope for salvation.

When the prayer ended, Truman gently squeezed her hand. The kindness softening his expression made her aware Tru offered silent solace and support to soothe her tears. Despite the kid gloves she wore, Sayra could feel the warmth of his touch and the abundance of his caring.

"Thanks for leading me back here, Sayra. I hope you'll join me here again." Eyes wet with unshed tears searched hers as he said, "We need to talk, Sayra. Would you have lunch with me?"

Half elation, half worry filled her. Were his tears a product of his prayers, or did they warn of some coming disappointment she could not sense at this moment?

Have but the faith of a mustard seed. The words raced

across her mind, and she quickly quelled her negative thoughts. "I'd love to, Truman, if you'll let it be mine and Lily's pleasure. Lily spent the morning cooking so we could invite you and Shago over after church."

"You cook?" Shago eyed Lily speculatively.

Challenge darkened her twilight-colored gaze to near purple. "Better than I sing."

"That good, huh?" He offered his arm. "Then I say we call it a truce and find out what we like about each other. We've already established what we don't particularly care for."

Lily linked her arm through his. "I don't know if I'll like much more about you when we get finished, but you're welcome to eat."

"Shall we?" Truman waited until Sayra accepted his lead. "I fear the forgiveness Brother Caleb's message suggested this morning may lose ground beneath Lily's honesty."

"I think it's most advisable," Sayra agreed, filing into the aisle to follow others out, "or there may not be any kitchen left by the time we get there. Those two need an armed chaperone."

As predicted by the moon's shadow last night, bad weather was setting in quickly. A misty dampness layered the air with a chill. Wind buffeted the ladies' bonnets and hems, billowing the men's Sunday frock coats behind them like great capes. Visiting on the church lawn was hurried. Politeness dictated each member remain long enough to personally greet the two newcomers, but introductions were brief. Invitations were accepted and given on both sides until finally all the families scurried off to seek shelter in their buggies and wagons.

The preacher finally had a moment to greet Sayra. When Truman introduced her, she assured him she and Lily would be back, then thanked him for the sermon. "I suppose everyone tells you they feel your sermon is aimed directly at them?"

The minister pressed his Bible against his heart. "Only if I'm fortunate enough to have done as good a job as the Lord expects of me."

"Well, you did one fine job this morning, Caleb." Truman slapped his friend good-naturedly on the back. "Sure made me do some thinking."

"Good, Tru. Thinking usually leads to doing. And the Lord prefers His children be doers. Can I expect to see you and Miss Martin at the Harvestfest this Wednesday? I need someone to drive the hay wagon and another to prepare something hot to drink."

"Tell you what, I'll fix the drinks," Tru thumbed toward Sayra. "She can drive the team."

Sayra smiled at his humor. The chill sank deeply into her bones, quaking through her and making her teeth chatter. "I t-take it, you've d-driven the hay wagon before for this event?"

Instinctively, Truman wrapped his arm around her shoulders, drawing Sayra closer to ward off the chill. Though a simple thoughtfulness, his intimate action warmed her blood.

"Being assigned the youth wagon would test the forebearance of Job. At least the children fall asleep on the way back. Our young ladies tend to giggle at every boast their beaux make. Then the boys spar for position next to the prettiest belle." Truman's laugh contained a hint of warning. "It makes for an interesting night, to say the least. What say I let you know by tomorrow, Brother Caleb? I need to check my schedule before I commit."

"Fair enough." Caleb shut the church door and offered to share the umbrella he opened above him. "Better get home soon. Looks like a real northwester coming in."

All three raced across the dirt road to the sheltered boardwalk. Caleb took refuge at the Osterman home while Truman and Sayra hurried on to the boarding house.

Since he never once let his arm drop from the protective warmth he offered, Sayra discovered how perfectly she fit at Truman's side. Their steps matched with no awkward bumping of hips affecting their stride. Her head fit in the crook of his shoulder, as if they were an extension of each other.

"Warm enough?"

His breath fanned across the top of her head. She looked up into eyes the color of emeralds. Sayra nodded, consumed with how natural their closeness seemed.

"Good, we're almost there."

He sounded almost relieved. Disappointment flashed through Sayra. Was this sense of belonging—*homecoming*—entirely one-sided? *Oh, ye of little faith*, she scolded, reminding herself how easily her commitment to believe swayed with every doubt.

When they reached the boarding house's elaborately carved doorway, Sayra stepped away from Truman and thanked him for his kindness.

"Purely my pleasure. Any time I can be of help, I'd like to do so." The smile he flashed her could have melted every peak on the snow-capped Rockies.

The door to the boarding house remained unlocked from dawn til midnight, allowing boarders easy access. Sayra invited Tru in, took his coat and hat, hung them on the rack in the foyer, then offered him a seat in the parlor.

Many of the guests were away visiting relatives, as was a common occurence on Sundays. Of those who remained, none sat in the bright yellow room filled with delicate white furniture, amber chandeliers, and Tiffany glass.

"Would you prefer to talk here or in the library?"

"Here's fine." Tru waited until Sayra chose a chair with a pattern of daisies sewn across its cushion, then he took a position on the settee fashioned in the same pattern and adjacent to her. His rugged frame overpowered the fragile-looking furniture. "Wouldn't want to get too comfortable, with what I have to say."

Immediately noticing the edge to his tone, Sayra fought to keep her hands from fidgeting. "What's on your mind?"

Truman sat back, attempted to find a relaxed position, couldn't, and ended up scooting to the edge of his seat. "Ever wondered why these contraptions were made for short-legged women? Give me a cowhide davenport any day."

With a sigh, Sayra stood. She'd been right. What Truman had to say must not be pleasant. Faith couldn't alter fact. . .could it? "We could move into the kitchen. I'll go see how much longer lunch will be."

Truman waved her back into her chair. "It's all right. I feel like a longhorn in a lady's shop no matter where I am anyway. I've worked outside stringing the wire so long, there's no refining me."

"That's where you're wrong, Truman. We all need a bit of molding, but you're one of the finest men I know." It felt good to speak her heart, and the expression that softened his face was worth every bit of nervousness she'd suffered while deciding to speak her mind.

"I'm glad you think so, Sayra." Their eyes met and held. "Because I wanted to tell you that I won't blame you if you never speak to me again."

"Whatever do you mean?" She'd never expected this.

"Well, like I said, I did a lot of thinking about what Caleb preached today. About asking for forgiveness. I'm ashamed to admit it, but I've treated you poorly since you arrived here." His hand reached out and she offered hers. A gentle squeeze to her fingertips punctuated his sincerity. "I had no right getting angry with you because you wouldn't tell me what forced you and Lily to leave Julesberg. That's your personal business. I'm sorry I overstepped those bounds and ask that you forgive my rudeness."

Sayra returned the squeeze, then let her hand return to her lap. "You have no reason to apologize. I'd say all you're guilty of is being concerned. It's I who should be begging your pardon. . .for not entrusting you with the truth."

"Powerful sermon, wasn't it?" Truman complimented.

"Hit me right in the guilty bone," she countered, "didn't it you?"

"That's how the best ones do." Respect washed over his rugged features. "They make you wanna up and right all your wrongs, change your ways, and believe life can be better for it."

"Do you mean that?" He'd offered her the perfect lead.

"Every word of it." Truman triangled his fingers in front of him. "Why?"

Let me say this right, Lord. Guide my words. "Because you do have a particular wrong you need to right, Truman. Life will be better for you if you can manage to forgive yourself."

Truman stood and walked over to the window that bayed in a half circle. Looking out past the brocade curtains into the watery-gray day, he whispered softly, "I can see I shared too much of my past with you, Miss Martin—but after all, it was only a game."

"With two very real players," she reminded gently. "But I think we both know we're not talking about our game of Taps, Truman. Don't you realize you can't go forward with your life until you admit you weren't really at fault for Ginny's leaving? Until you absolve yourself for her death, you'll always be tapping out the same message over and over again. . .with not enough wire strung from here to eternity to answer your cry for help."

He turned his back on her. "I'd rather not discuss this."

"Why? Because it's too hard to face the truth?" Sayra moved toward him, reaching out to touch and offer solace. "Forgive yourself, Truman, so you can get on with living. No matter how hard you tried, Ginny would always have run. Deep down I believe you know that. What I don't understand is why you want to continue to suffer."

Truman jerked away from her touch, his eyes narrowing. "What gives you the right to stand there and make such an accusation, to tell me what I'm feeling or thinking?"

Sayra's hand dropped to her side. Suddenly she felt colder than she'd been outside, yet truth rushed to defend her actions and spread a warmth through her. "Because I'm willing to wait on you. I have the courage to deliver the message of truth I'm feeling at the moment."

"W-What?" He looked as if he'd been struck by a boulder.

"That frightens you, doesn't it, Truman? Finally someone is willing to care for you when you can't even care for yourself and allow you all the time in the world you need to come to terms with the past."

He began to pace the room like a caged bobcat. "You don't know what you're saying. What you're offering."

"Don't I?" She fell in step alongside him, matching him stride for stride. "It means you don't have to prove anything to me, run after me, give up your dream with the telegraph. You don't have to nurture the guilt that you fell short with Ginny, simply because you're afraid you can't live up to what *you* expect of yourself. It's easier to hide behind the falsehood of past neglect you aren't guilty of than face the challenge of loving someone now. . .today, isn't it?"

Growing stone silent, he stopped and stubbornly folded his arms across his chest. She did the same. "All you have to do is give your cares to God. Let Him be the judge. A simple thing really. Lay it all out on the altar. Give your past to God and let Him make you new." Her voice hushed as she fought for control of the turmoil of emotions surging inside her. "Trust me to be your friend, if nothing else."

"Friends trust friends."

She didn't have to ask why his eyes glared with accusal. Sayra knew its source. "You're right, of course. I was wrong not telling you about the real reason I left Julesberg. But at the time, I hadn't laid down my burden myself, either. It took a visit to a very special place in the mountains with a miner who's probably seen more of heaven than just about anyone I know. Then this morning, when I heard Shago sing, I realized we all have talents meant especially for us. And if Shago's could be developed so beautifully, then perhaps I could find my own and do the same. After hearing Brother Caleb's sermon, I finally realized that those decisions I'd made led me straight to here and what I'm feeling now. Maybe that wasn't such a bad thing, after all. Especially if you can forgive me for leaving Julesberg in the manner I did."

"You don't need my approval for anything you do."

She sat on the settee and patted the cushion beside her. "It's not your approval I'm wanting, but your understanding. Will you join me?"

"Lunch should be ready soon, shouldn't it?"

Always the clock-watcher, this man she cared for. "I'll make this brief."

He sat, deliberately scooting to the far edge of the settee, folded his arms across his chest, and leaned backward, building a physical wall of resistance to anything she had to say. "Proceed."

"You remember the story you heard about how Parker Quinton got hurt?" He nodded. "Well, all that's true. But the real reason I left was because I was afraid my brother-in-law, Ulysses, would come take Lily away from me." When Sayra finished confiding all her misdirected good intentions, she awaited Truman's reactions.

Would he think her choices frivolous, or would he realize, just as she had, that each choice led her to *this* moment, this effort to help him as well as herself?

Laughter erupted from the other end of the settee— the last reaction she expected. Heat suffused her cheeks. Anger ignited in the pit of her stomach and raced through Sayra like wildfire. She jolted to her feet. Not a single moment since leaving Port Hudson had been anything to joke about. "Why are you laughing?" she demanded.

Truman wiped a sleeve across his eyes as merriment brought moisture to them. "You don't understand. I'm not laughing at *you*. I'm thinking how ironic this all is. Parker Quinton thought he'd had a turn of good luck when you two decided to leave. He thought he could move those supplies you saw in the barn before anyone else found out about them. Instead, his commanding officer got wind of his activities and launched a full investigation. You see, the major had been pilfering company supplies and selling them to the Paiutes."

Though laughter still brightened his eyes, Tru's expression sobered. "Had Quinton let things be and not tried to worm his way out of trouble, no one would have gotten wise to the fact that he'd been hording supplies that didn't belong to him."

"What supplies?" When Sayra attempted to recall seeing anything out of the ordinary in the barn, only the smell of old hay, aged leather, and dust wafted through her memory.

"You didn't see them?"

"No, and Lily didn't say anything—" Realization swept through Sayra. "You found them in the loft, didn't you?"

"I didn't say that!" Lily interrupted, entering the parlor as if she'd been waiting in the foyer for a cue. But there was little doubt where she'd spent her time since leaving church. From the top of her head to the bottom of her kid boots, she was dusted in flour.

"You never mentioned anything about finding supplies in the loft of that old barn in Julesberg," Sayra urged.

Lily wiped her hands on the apron tied around her blue calico dress. "Oh, that. I thought maybe the army was using it as an extra warehouse. You know, like Papa does sometimes with our cotton."

The sight of her niece finally became a more important issue than the supplies. "Why on earth do you look like that, Lily Jane Van Buren?"

"Because *I* look like *this*," Shago announced, nudging Lily so she was forced to move to one side of the entryway. Dark brown stains splattered his face, hair, and Sunday-Go-to-Meeting clothes so badly that the original butternut-colored trousers looked like leopard skin.

Lily's chin lifted jauntily as her gaze slanted menacingly toward Shago. "Lunch is served."

fourteen

Because she was restless and wanted to keep her hands busy, Sayra helped Lily clean up the dishes. As she put the plates on the top shelf, she couldn't get Truman's last words from her mind. Since that first service spent together, they'd shared three Sundays sitting in the Taylor pew and having lunch afterward. Yet she remained confused about his feelings toward her.

This morning, after a frustrating attempt to get him to talk about something more than their work, he apologized and said perhaps another time. He explained that a grizzly had chosen a handful of telegraph poles to mark his territory yesterday and decided to use them as backscratchers.

What could she say to his legitimate excuse for leaving? Truman had to get the line up again.

But it was the last statement he made which both pleased and worried her. "I need a bit of time to think some things through."

The back door to the kitchen blew open, sending a blast of cold whirling air around the room, rattling pots and pans that hung on the wall.

"Close the door!" Lily turned her face away to shield herself from the blast.

"What's the matter, fair maiden? Cold too much for you?" Shago entered, dusting the snow from his hat and coat. "A pity. I came to see if you'd like to go for a sleigh ride with me."

"A sleigh ride!" Lily's anger became anticipation as she laid down her drying towel. "Oh, Aunt Sayra, do you suppose I could?" She glanced around at the remaining dishes and frowned. "But then, I couldn't leave you with the rest of this. It isn't fair."

"We'll all do them," Shago announced, starting forward.

"Stop right there, young man!" Sayra demanded. "Don't move another inch. You'll track mud on these floors."

Shago took several steps backward. "Ooooh, sorry. I forgot I'd stumbled in that slush near the back door. Give me a minute to take my boots off and I'll help."

"No," Sayra shooed Lily out of the kitchen, "let her go get warm gloves and a heavy coat. I'll finish these up while you two go have that lovely ride. The mountains are beautiful this morning. I could hardly concentrate on the sermon for looking outside the windows to stare at them."

"Thanks, Aunt Sayra." Lily kissed Sayra's cheeks and rushed away to dress warmly.

Sayra poured a container of hot apple cider and took two cups from the shelves. "Here. This was left over from breakfast, and the guests have already had their fill."

"Thanks." He took the offered items. "Sure you don't want to go with us?"

Though his words included her in the outing, Shago could not hide the truth in his expression. He planned on courting Lily today. Ever since the flour-chocolate fight in the kitchen that first Sunday he and Lily had sung together, they had become nearly inseparable. They bickered and beleaguered one another, yet neither had eyes for anyone else. Whether or not Lily or Shago realized the truth, both Sayra and Truman recognized the love blossoming between the pair.

"No, I'd rather not," she said truthfully. "Perhaps Truman will finish early and come on in. I'd like to have a hot meal waiting on him when he does."

"That's kind of you, but he's working about a couple of miles west of town. It's slow going in this snow. His hands will get too cold to work at times. Then when he does get done, it'll be a long trek back."

"I'll wait nevertheless."

"How do I look?" Lily rushed into the kitchen, dressed in a coat and heavy wool dress the shade of lilacs in full bloom.

"Prettier than an angel," Shago whispered reverently, then realized what he'd said and quickly acted nonchalant. "But I've had occasions to lock horns with you, so don't go trying to tempt me. . .I know the truth."

"You two go on and have a good time." Sayra adjusted Lily's fur-lined bonnet and checked to see that each button of her coat was securely fastened. "Good, you got your warm gloves. It's already three o'clock. I want you home long before nightfall. Agreed?"

"We will be," Shago assured her as he opened the door once more to let in a wintry blast. "Don't worry about us. I'm going to take her up to the lake and back. We should be gone about an hour."

As the frosty air stung Sayra's cheeks, sending a shiver through her that made standing in the doorway near impossible, she called after them, "That cider will only stay warm for a little while. Have fun and be careful."

Sayra closed the door and peered through the curtain, watching as Shago lifted Lily into the sleigh. His hands lingered as he placed her in the seat. Lily smiled down at him adoringly and laughed at something he said. Her niece had certainly come into her own since meeting the boy. The quick intelligence Sayra often caught glimpses of in Lily flourished daily beneath Shago's growing respect for her.

"Slow down," Sayra whispered, watching Shago nearly fall as he reached around the back of the sleigh to get to the driver's side. Taking a seat beside Lily, he grabbed the reins and waved at Sayra. Lily turned and did the same.

Sayra's gaze raced over her niece, taking in every detail. Gloves. Kid boots laced high. Layers of petticoats beneath her wool dress. A heavy coat and bonnet, lined with wool. *She's warm enough*, Sayra assured herself, struggling to shake off a sense of foreboding. *You're being too protective.*

A quick survey of Shago's attire revealed he wasn't taking any chances either. He spread a blanket across Lily's lap and another one over himself. The horses looked sturdy as he flicked them into motion. Still, Sayra watched until the sleigh was but a mere speck on the horizon.

A shiver raced through her, and she supposed a cup of coffee might warm away the chill. After preparing a new pot, she decided the best way to occupy herself until everyone returned was to cook the roast she'd planned. "That will keep my hands busy, sure enough," she said aloud to the potholder designed with a cow in its center. "But what about my mind? How am I going to stop worrying 'til all three of them are in out of the cold?"

❧

"Brrrr! It's cold enough to freeze brimstone!" Truman said to the big Belgian. "Good thing this is the last pole. Don't know if I could have lasted much longer."

The horse snorted, letting out a billowing cloud of frosty air from his nostrils. He sidestepped, making the harness jingle and jolting the wagon into motion.

"Whoa, boy. Don't take off just yet." Truman talked in soothing tones to the animal, trying to calm him. "That's all I'd need."

The animal bobbed his head up and down, then shook it back and forth as if unable to make up his mind. Truman connected the last wire, all the while watching the steed for any indication he might bolt. Being this far from town so late in the evening made survival in this weather depend upon the horse.

His hand instantly jerked back as the wire began to hum. "Must have been sitting there waiting for me to finish," he joked. "Can't get it done fast enough for them, fella."

Truman started shinnying down the pole when he stopped mid-slide. That was the Georgetown code. The office was closed on Sunday. There shouldn't have been anyone manning the key.

Certainty filled him. There was trouble of some sort. He only prayed it didn't involve someone he knew or loved. Though exhausted from hours working in the cold, Truman climbed the pole as if the grizzly had returned for a bit of backscratching. He tapped in and began to listen to the emergency ticking out over the line.

"Guide me!" he shouted to his Maker as he deciphered the message. A glance down into the wagon said it would take more time to rig up a set of keys to telegraph his answer back than it would to be on his way. He reconnected the wire to enable it to send on to other points west and prayed Sayra would understand that he made the only choice he could at the time.

"Got to find them," he spoke his fear to the Belgian, wondering if he should unhitch the horse or take the wagon as well. He opted for the latter, thinking he'd best prepare for the worst. "Maybe they aren't hurt." He jumped into the driver's seat and flicked the Belgian into motion. "Come on, boy, you've been wanting to get home. Hyaahh."

❧

Sayra felt her hysteria rising with every plod of the horse's hooves. The going was achingly slow. The horse was unable to move quickly in the knee-deep snow. She searched the horizon, praying the image of a sleigh would appear, but no matter how desperately she searched, the image never came.

Others searched with her. She had enlisted the help of everyone in the congregation who lived in town, the deputy, and their landlady. The men gathered up lanterns. A single pistol shot rent the air again, the signal they'd agree upon to try to rouse Shago's and Lily's attention if they were still alive. Sayra halted, listening, praying a volley of three shots would follow, relaying the message that the sleigh and its occupants had been found.

Nothing. Cold, blinding silence.

She kicked the horse into motion again, reining toward a nearby aspen. With two slashes, Sayra carved a cross in the trunk, marking a return path as she had since becoming separated from the others in the dark. Unskilled at handling a weapon, she had foolishly relied on someone else being around to signal if she happened across the missing youths. Now, Sayra wished she'd been wiser.

Onward the horse plodded, until time seemed to cease and the cold became a white shroud of doom.

ॐ

Her eyes blinked open as the horse halted beneath her. Sayra was startled to realize she'd fallen asleep in the saddle. Though the sun had long since set, moonlight glinted off the snow, lighting the night with a million twinkling stars.

The horse snorted and wouldn't move forward, his ears twitching and muscles bunching beneath her. "What is it, boy?" She searched the ground below her for signs of what spooked him.

The land ahead rose sharply. . .almost too sharply. The horse must have sensed danger; Sayra could feel its fear beneath her. "Back up real slow, fella," she crooned softly, trying to soothe him. "Over here now. Yes, this way. That's right. That'a boy. Slowly. . .slowly . . .well-done, big fella. Well-done."

As he continued to back more, his feet slid. Horse and rider threatened to topple. He attempted to rear, but couldn't. "Steady, boy. Steady!" Sayra clung to his neck as hard as her cold hands would allow, whispering desperately into his ear, fighting the urge to shout, for it would only frighten him further.

Finally the slide stopped. The animal steadied on his feet. His muscles quivered beneath her as he stood on trembling legs. "You did it, fella," she soothed. "You're all right now."

Keeping a close hold on the reins, she dismounted and gave the animal a minute to regain its sense of well-being. Looking back to see what may have frightened him further, horror gripped her lungs and made breathing near impossible. The sleigh, turned over. Two huddled forms lay unconscious. . .or worse. . .dead.

Quickly hobbling her own mount so it wouldn't be able to go far, she rushed over to allay her dread. A fast inspection found a steady pulse at Lily's throat, but Shago's was weak, at best. From the angle of his leg lying beneath the horses that had pulled the sleigh, she suspected it was broken in several places. A dark stain surrounded the snow where Shago lay, and she feared he might have lost too much blood.

"Help somebody! Help!" she screamed, praying someone in the search party would hear her. "I've found them and they're hurt. Over here!"

No one answered. Realizing she couldn't wait for help to reach her, Sayra whispered, "I've got to move you, Shago. I don't want to, but if Lily can help, I need her." With all her might, she tugged him sideways, flinching at the sound of his deep moan, praying that God would help her in this needy hour.

"Lily, wake up! Shago's badly hurt. He needs us. Lily, you've got to help, honey."

Her efforts roused her niece. Lily's eyes opened,

bringing with them a glazed look and finally recognition.

"The horses slipped," she murmured. "Shago's trying to get them up, but they won't stand. Can you help him?"

"Listen to me very carefully, Lily." Sayra spoke her words precisely and as loud as her trembling voice could muster. "Shago's hurt bad. If we don't free him, he'll bleed to death. Do you understand, Lily?"

"Shago hurt?" She rose, moaned, and grabbed her head. A glance at the man lying beside her in the snow evoked a scream. "Oh, Lord, please no! No!"

"Help me, Lil. We've got to move this horse." If only she didn't have such an objection to carrying a gun, she could have signaled for help and put the poor team out of its misery.

Rising unsteadily to her feet, Lily stepped cautiously around Shago. Even with their combined effort, the women didn't have enough strength to free him.

"What are we going to do?" Lily asked, returning to Shago's side and bending to place his head in her lap. She smoothed hair from his forehead as tears trickled down her cheeks. "We can't just let him die."

"Here, take this and wrap it around him." Sayra removed her coat and handed it to Lily. A bone-chilling cold made her flinch. None of them could last much longer out here. "I'm going to see if my horse can pull away the mare that has Shago pinned."

Sayra worked for what seemed a long time, but proved to be only minutes. Though her mount shied from the smell of death, she used Shago's knife to cut the reins on the sleigh, knot them together, and attach them to her own saddle, creating a tow line.

Keeping traction beneath the horse's hooves proved to be the most difficult obstacle she faced. Several times Sayra fell, once landing flat on her face and breaking open her lip. Cold bit into the cut, stabbing her with pain, but Sayra didn't worry about her own needs. Shago was close to passing over. Finally she had no choice but to ask for the coat she'd given Lily. Placing it on the ice in front of the horse, she urged him forward. One step, then two. The animal didn't slide. Third hoof. Fourth. The towline moved its cargo an inch.

Sayra repeated the painstaking progress, constantly throwing the coat in front of her mount after its back hooves worked their way forward enough to move the dead weight an inch or more.

Shago moaned constantly, apparently in extreme pain. Sayra hurt in places she didn't know she had muscles, but still she continued to tug and tow.

Please God, let someone find us, she prayed, wondering how long her strength would hold out. Her mouth hurt. Every muscle ached. Her feet and hands were so cold, they tingled from the onset of numbness. *Someone strong enough to pull this horse off Shago*, she added selfishly. *Don't let him die because of my weakness*.

"Help us," she yelled so fiercely pain gripped her throat. But her shouts were in vain. She openly wept now, allowing the anger that brimmed inside her to well. "You promised if I believed, I would receive," she challenged, yet quickly asked that He forgive her for allowing her fear to become anger. "You said if I but asked, You would hear." Her eyes searched the night, looking for any sign of her Maker's presence, finding nothing but the cold, white glare of death staring back.

In hoarse supplication, she bowed her head and whispered, "Jesus said You already know our needs, Lord. That all we have to say is Your prayer. Well, I can't seem to find any better words. And if I could, I wouldn't know if they're the *right* ones. 'Our Father who art in heaven, hallowed by Thy name. Thy kingdom. . . .'"

Lily's sweet voice joined hers, broken by sobs.

The wind howled fiercely, as if laughing at their frailty.

"Lillllly! Shagoooo! Where are youooo?" The wind mocked again as it grew in fury.

"Did you hear that?" Sayra asked.

"Hear what?" Lily craned her ear in the direction her aunt pointed. "Was it angels?"

"Lily! Shago! Where are you?" The voice drew closer. "Lily! Sha—"

"Over here!" Sayra shouted, waving frantically to the horse and wagon taking shape in the distance. "Over here! Thank God, oh, thank God!" She raced to Lily. "Stand up, Lily. Let's shout together and wave our hands so whoever it is will see us better."

Lily gently laid Shago's head back in the snow and began waving and shouting at the top of her lungs. The sight of the large horse and wagon filled Sayra with hope. Together, they could pull the dead weight the rest of the way off. The wagon could carry them all back into Georgetown.

"God bless you!" she shouted as the driver flicked the horse into a faster gait. Finally he reined the wagon up short and jumped from the buckboard. Sayra blinked several times, her lashes near frozen together with frost, trying to focus on the guardian angel she knew beyond a shadow of a doubt had been God's gift to them in their hour of need. The man's form took substance, and he thumbed back his hat.

"Sayra, thank goodness you found them."

"Truman!" She wept with relief as she flung her arms around him. "You heard the wire. I sent you message after message, but there was no answer. Yet you heard it. Shago's hurt bad. He needs your help."

Sayra pulled away quickly from the comfort of Tru's embrace and began to explain what they must do or risk losing his brother.

Later she would tell Truman what her heart confided at the sight of him. Later, when Shago wasn't fighting for his life. "God, give us strength," she prayed.

fifteen

Truman paced the floor of the doctor's office for more than two hours, waiting, praying for the operation to be complete.

"I need to see Shago!" he demanded, unable to endure another moment of not knowing whether his brother would awaken from the surgery.

Sayra rose from her chair and went to him. "You can't right now, Truman. Doc says what we need is time."

"I have to talk to him." Truman despised the lack of control he felt. He'd always managed to take care of Shago, being there to comfort at every fall or each scuffed knee. Now when his brother needed him most, why did he feel so helpless?

"The doctor will let you see him in the morning, when Shago's been through the worst of it." Sayra tried to be kind but firm. "He won't be able to hear you now, anyway. He's had a lot of laudanum."

Truman wanted to scream. "Why Shago, Sayra? Why not me instead? He's only seventeen."

Gently, Sayra rested her hand on his shoulder and led him to a cot the doctor had set up in one corner for family members of overnight patients. "Come rest here, Tru. Close your eyes awhile, and I'll watch for you. You should be rested when he comes around. He'll need you even more then."

"If he does." Truman collapsed on the cot, his body

153

and mind too tense to sleep. His eyes closed abruptly. "I didn't mean that, Lord. I'm just so tired. Take care of him, please."

"Here." Sayra held out a jar.

"My mustard seed! When did you. . . ?" Truman clutched the jar as if it were a lifeline and he were drowning.

"When I ran over to the office this morning and left the note explaining why there wouldn't be any business today." Sayra glanced at the closed door that barred them from Shago. "Sometimes I need a reminder of how little faith it takes for a miracle to occur. Thought you might just need one, too."

Truman's heart felt heavy with a battery of emotions. Words failed him. He simply reached out, took her hand in his, and pressed a kiss into her palm. "More so now than ever before. Believe with me, Sayra. Help me replant the seed."

❧

Hours moved slowly. Finally the door to Shago's room opened. Though his face looked haggard, the light of miracles shone from Doc's eyes. He gave a silent nod. Truman was at Shago's bedside within seconds.

"Hello, Shakespeare." Truman forced the worry from his tone. He hoped his face didn't show all he'd been through the past ten hours. The kid could read him as easily as a first-grade primer.

Shago opened his eyes, staring blankly at his brother. "Truman?" His voice was raw and hoarse from being exposed to the elements for too long.

"In the flesh," Truman answered, reaching for Shago's hand. "Didn't think I'd be anywhere else 'til you came around, did you?"

"Sayra manning the line?"

"No, she's waiting to see you. Lily, too."

"No, not Lily." His gray eyes focused. . .demanded. "Whatever you do, don't let her see me like this."

"It's just a. . ." No matter which way he tried to say it, his words would be abrasive. Truman left them unsaid.

"What. . .a leg? Say it, Tru. It's real. We can't hide it." He slung back the sheet. "I no longer have two legs. A fact I have to live with. Don't go tiptoeing around me. Just say it like it is. Like we always have. I don't want to be treated any differently. I don't need any coddling."

"I won't." Truman bowed his head. "Never again, I promise."

"Good, now there's something you can do for me." He spread the covers over the lower half of his body. "I want you to see that Lily doesn't need for anything. Keep an eye on her and her aunt for me."

"You can do that yourself. You'll be up and around in no time. This won't affect your job any, except you may have to wait a little while before shinnying up any poles."

Shago nodded. "And I'll do that again, someday. You mark my words. But Lily. . .that's a different situation, all together. She's so feisty and full of spunk. She needs to go on and marry a man who can chase her around the furniture and give her a dozen or so kids. I can't tie her to a cripple."

"Why don't you let *me* be the judge of that?" Lily marched into the room like a temperance leader at a saloon owners' meeting.

"Get out of here!" Shago demanded, plunging his head into his pillow.

"I can yell just as loud as you can, Shago Jones. I have four brothers to argue with. You only have one." Lily grabbed the edge of the sheet. "So stop acting like a spoiled child and look at me."

"What are you doing?" Shago's head spun around as he glared at her.

Challenge flared in her eyes. "Do you think it matters one tiny bit to me that you have one leg instead of two? I'll probably turn as red as Truman's bandanna there, but don't think I won't look."

"Don't lift that sheet."

Truman scooted away, sensing that Lily had his brother completely under control and spellbound despite himself.

"Why not? If missing a leg is going to keep you from wanting to be my friend, then don't I have a right to see why?"

"Lily, I'm not dressed beneath these covers!"

Lily willingly released it.

Anquish guided Shago. "I'm no longer a whole man, Lily."

Her fists knotted on her hips as she rocked back on her heels. "So you're going to just lie there in a bed for the rest of your life and feel sorry for yourself?"

His face turned red with rage. "What do you expect from me? Leave me alone!"

"Come on, Lily," Sayra suggested quietly, tugging on her niece's arm. "Perhaps now isn't the time."

"Now is exactly the time, Aunt Sayra." Lily refused to move. Grabbing Shago's fist, she tugged on his fingers until they reluctantly splayed open and allowed her to place her own there. Her gaze demanded his and received it. "I'll tell you why I won't leave you alone,

Shago Jones. A lot of people think I'm slow. I've even been called simple-minded. And maybe I am, according to their way of thinking. But you know what? Not one single time since I've been on this earth has God ever made me feel crippled in my mind. Not one single time."

Shago rushed to defend her. "You're *not* simple-minded, Lil. You're a lot more quick-witted than I can ever keep up with."

Lily flashed a wide smile. "So you see. . .we're both whole in the Lord's eyes. It doesn't matter to Him what anyone else thinks of us, as long as what's inside here," she pressed her hand to her heart, "is love. What's a leg or being a little slow matter when we've got each other?"

Gray eyes misted over, then closed as Shago whispered, "You never said you loved me."

She pressed a kiss on the back of his hand. "How could I not love the only man who's ever been simple enough to treat me like I was smarter than he is? A girl's gotta stop and count her blessings when she finds someone that kind."

Truman touched Sayra's shoulder and nodded toward the door. A glance at Doc said he understood. They silently moved into the next room, aware that the young couple had forgotten everyone else in the room at the moment.

"Guess that young man will heal sure enough, now that Miss Lily's set her hat for him." Doc rolled down his sleeves and buttoned them.

The deep sigh that escaped Truman drained the worry that had kept him wound tight as a three-day clock during the hours of pacing the floor. Suddenly he felt weary, but it was a good exhaustion. Things would be fine again. Shago would not give up on living; his brother had the love of a good woman to see to that.

The love of a good woman. Tru's gaze was drawn to Sayra. God bless her, she'd done everything within human power to save Shago's life. And when that failed, Lily said Sayra had prayed heaven down for a miracle. Tru picked up the jar from the cot where he'd left it. The mustard seed was small, indeed, but it had been Sayra's giant faith that saved his brother's life and kept Tru believing. Her faith had helped him not to lose hope.

"Would you walk with me to the office, Sayra? I'd like to send a telegram."

Sayra gathered her coat and asked Doc if he would let Lily know where she'd be. "Can't it wait until to-morrow, Tru? You're so exhausted."

"No, this message can't wait a moment longer."

Truman asked her to wait while he had a moment alone with his brother and Lily. When he returned, Tru bade the doctor good-day and said they would look in on Shago in a few hours. Truman evaded Sayra's questions as he hurried her down the street.

Upon entering, he discovered the stove needed to heat. Tru set about building a fire while Sayra attempted to keep warm by rubbing her gloved hands together.

"If there's any water left in that pitcher, would you make some coffee?" He pointed to the washstand near the stove. "That way we'll have something warm to sip when the fire gets going."

"S-Sure," Sayra said through chattering teeth. "Hope the keys aren't frozen up. Though my fingers are so cold, I doubt they could send a message right now anyway."

Truman finished his task quickly, setting the coffee pot atop the stove.

"Take off your gloves, Sayra," he said.

Slowly she pulled her chilly fingers from the leather and bent her knuckles to get her blood circulating.

Without a word, Truman reached for her hands and rubbed them between his warm palms. A simple gesture that any friend might do for another, but his actions made Sayra blush.

"Are you ready to send that message now?" he asked.

Sayra dropped her chin so that he could not see the depth of her emotions in her eyes and nodded. Her fingers still tingled as she sat down in front of the telegraph key. . .not from numbness now, but from Truman's touch.

"Final station?"

"Port Hudson," Truman informed.

Her gaze immediately rose to meet his. Her voice became hushed and hesitant. "Receiver?"

"Mr. Ulysses Van Buren."

Sayra's fingers paused over the keys. "What are you going to tell—"

"Remember the first rule of transmission, Miss Martin. Your job is to take the message, not change its contents."

At his gentle reprimand, her cheeks already dusted a rosy hue, deepened in color.

Patience, love, he silently whispered. *You said you would wait for me. I'm holding you to your promise.*

"Dear Mr. Van Buren. Stop. Wanted to be the first to congratulate you on the impending marriage of your daughter, Miss Lily Van Buren, to my younger brother, Shago Jones. Stop. Please be informed that one month from today, the proud couple will be married in the First Christian Church of Georgetown, Colorado.

Brother Caleb MacAllister, officiating. Stop—"

A smile spread across Sayra's lips as she comprehended what his moment alone with Shago and Lily had yielded.

"—We hope that you, Mrs. Van Buren, and the children will be able to attend. Stop. Don't worry about arrangements other than travel. Stop. The Western Union will have accommodations awaiting you upon arrival. Stop." Truman watched the keys move rapidly beneath Sayra's fingers. When they halted, he sat in the chair opposite the desk, leaning closer. "Tap out like I usually do. Truman Taylor, Southwest Supernumerary, Western Union, etc. . . . ."

Sayra completed the message, then looked up, realizing he stared at her. "Is that all?"

"No. There's another."

Reluctantly, she turned back to the machine. Her fingers posed, ready for instruction.

"To Bess Van Buren." When the clicks finished, Truman took his courage in hand and began: "Seldom does a man get the privilege of meeting a fine Christian woman here in the west. Your sister, Sayra, is such a woman. Stop."

The becoming blush he'd instigated moments ago blossomed, sweeping up her neck and spilling out onto Sayra's cheeks.

"Rarely does a man find one with the courage to face the impossible, yet never give up. Thanks to your Sayra, my brother is alive and thrilled to be the proud intended husband of your lovely daughter. Stop."

Truman felt as if he'd passed the reins that had been tightly holding his heart over to Sayra at this moment. The love that echoed in her eyes gave him permission to run free. "Never have I known a woman so selfless in her actions, so eager to commit a kindness. One more willing to forgive shortcomings than bring them to our attention. A woman wise enough to teach me how to forgive myself as well as others. But more importantly. . ."

The clicks stopped. She waited patiently. She had said she would wait for him forever. Truman could see that forever shining in her eyes. ". . .a woman who's made me believe that love, like heaven, is eternal. I pray she will become *my* Sayra. Stop."

He wasn't certain what he expected, but certainly not what followed. Sayra turned abruptly and began to tap so fast he could hardly decipher the code. It seemed a request for items to be brought with the family. Something old. Something new. A lacy hanky to be borrowed from an aunt. Bess's wedding dress was to be packed for Lily and their mother's as well for. . .her!

A smile showered his face with happiness. He nearly dropped his chair as he jolted to his feet. "I take it this means you'll marry me?"

Sayra held up a single finger and silently asked him to wait. With slow deliberate strokes she tapped out a single word, *Yes*.

Truman closed the distance between them, moving the machine aside. Taking her in his arms, his lips lowered to Sayra's until they were but a breath away. The sight of her injured mouth halted his kiss. Lifting her chin with one knuckle, he said with great patience, "We'll have to wait, but I promise it'll be spectacular."

"Like your method of proposing?" She laughed and pressed a palm to his cheek. "A month doesn't seem half as long as forever to wait for another of your spectaculars."

sixteen

Though there were a multitude of details to take care of, the month seemed to last forever. An invitation was sent via the stage to Aud Williams, Turk, and Mrs. Koumalapalous. The ladies auxiliary at the church insisted on planning a reception that kept Sayra busy simply trying to appease each woman's suggestion.

Most of Lily's time was spent at Shago's side while he recuperated. During the past week, he'd insisted upon trying his hand at crutches. Despite Tru's and Sayra's protests that he would be taking an unnecessary risk, in no way did Shago plan to await his bride from a wheelchair. He planned to stand beside her, even if it meant leaning on crutches.

Though Tru and Sayra worried over the falls he took, Lily helped him up each time and told him how much better that try was than the last one. Shago simply wiped his brow, said all the fuss was "much ado about nothing," then attempted to walk farther.

Sayra's lip healed within two weeks, but Truman had not attempted to kiss her. . .no matter how she tried to persuade him to do so. Asking him to wipe the cake batter from her lips yesterday morning hadn't worked. And last week's comment by Doc that she had a clean bill of health flew right past Truman, to her great chagrin.

When disappointment threatened to become hurt,

162

Truman reminded her that she'd promised to wait on him. And wait they would, he said, until they sealed their marriage with the first of many kisses in the sight of God.

Though she pouted, secretly Sayra was thrilled at Truman's game of cat and mouse. Their relationship had started with Taps, and their future promised not only to be as "spectacular" as he promised, but worth the wait.

"They're here!" Lily shouted, flinging the door open and letting in the gust of warm air the unusual winter day had blessed them with. For a week now, the snow had melted, leaving only patches here and there to remind them of last month's storms. "I saw Jimmy Don and the boys riding shotgun with the driver. Poor soul, I bet he'll be glad to deliver these passengers."

Sayra grabbed her niece's hand and raced outside. Their legs didn't stop until they brought them to a halt in front of the stage station, where Sayra yearned for the first sight of her beloved sister.

"Lily!" four voices shouted in unison. "Aunt Sayra! Look Momma and Papa. It's Lily."

Lily opened her arms wide, and eight gangly arms flung themselves around her as her four brothers squeezed until she had to beg them to let go long enough for her to catch her breath.

The door to the stage swung open and Ulysses stepped out. Before any greetings could be given, he turned immediately and offered help to his wife as she exited the stage.

"Sayra, darling. How good it is to see you."

Bess hugged Sayra so fiercely Sayra feared she

would suffer a stiff neck if her sibling didn't let go soon. "Sis, it's been so long. My, but haven't you grown lovelier by the day!"

"Mama!"

Excitement filled Lily's voice, making Sayra step aside to let mother and daughter embrace.

"Lily, my love. Let me look at you." When Lily finally stepped back, tears shown in Bess's blue eyes. "Oh my, how you've grown. You're no longer Mama's little girl, are you? You've developed into a lovely young lady these past few months. A soon-to-be *married* young woman."

"Euuuwww. Married." Jimmy Don's nose wrinkled up into a mass of freckles.

"Lily's getting hitched, Lily's getting hitched," sing-songed Eddie Mack, the second-oldest of the boys.

"Since I'm the oldest now, can I have your room?" Thomas Wayne asked with anticipation. "My salamander likes to sleep under your bed."

Sayra laughed. "You're all definitely the same. All boys."

Ulysses stood behind his brood, keeping silent until the women had time for the hellos to wear off. "Where's my about-to-be son-in-law?"

"At the church." Lily moved away from her mother and held her arms out to her father.

With an anguished cry he rushed to her, threw his arms about her, and lifted her off the ground. Ulysses twirled her around and finally set Lily back on her feet. "My little girl! How I've missed you these many months. But then," his voice broke, "you aren't a baby any more, like your mother says. You're full grown."

His hand reached out to gently rub her cheek. "Can you ever forgive me? I should have taken more time . . .been more patient with you. . .protected you from those ruffians."

Lily pressed a kiss upon his cheek and smiled at him. "Papa, I already forgave you. And you weren't so busy you couldn't come to my wedding."

He hugged her fiercely, unashamedly releasing tears. Finally he looked up and realized that all stared at him and Lily with silly grins on their faces. . .Sayra's the biggest of all. In a voice deliberately gruff, he attempted to regain his normal stoic expression. "Lead me to this young man, so I—your mother and I—can have a moment with him before we hand over our pride and joy to him."

"Dad-blamed-fangled-good-for-nothing—"

Bess stepped to the stage door and peered in. "Now, Miss Williams, you promised you wouldn't use that language in front of the children."

"—bloomers." A hemline of five petticoats beneath a silver taffeta gown announced the presence of the fussing passenger as she attempted to get out of the stage. "All these buttons and bows and lacy thangs are just about enough to make a woman wanta stay poor. Sorry, Mrs. Van Buren, but these garments got me so riled, I'm about to spit vinegar." The ermine-colored ringlets beneath the silver bonnet were as startlingly familiar as the voice and choice of words. "Aud!" Sayra yelled, racing to hug the miner. "You came. And as a woman!"

Puzzled looks passed between Ulysses and Bess.

"Well, don't that beat all." Aud threw her arms

around Sayra and Lily at the same time. "Said I would, didn't I? When did I ever break my word to the likes of Miss Lily. . .or anyone else for that matter?"

"Frills and lace, you promised sure enough," Lily reminded. "And don't you just look beautiful!"

"I had a better chance at beauty before me and that stagecoach tangled. Used to riding shotgun up with Ol' Waylay there. Thought I was going to have to hibernate for the winter before it let me a-loose." Aud eyed Lily with affection. "Maybe you better get that upcoming husband of yours to buy you a pair of spectacles for a wedding present, child. I'm a far sight from perty."

"Plum fetching's what she is," said the long-necked man who exited behind her. "What say we all move away from the stage so's we can uncramp these old legs?"

Aud turned and grabbed hold of the man's arm. "Sayra, Miss Lily, you'd be to remembering Turkelrod."

"Why, it is you, Turk!" Lily eyed him a bit closer and sniffed. "And you smell lots better, too."

"Lily!" Sayra and Bess scolded in unison.

"Well it seems we're all here," Ulysses reminded, his impatience growing. "Since further introductions here are no longer necessary, what say we meet your two young men?"

"First, let's get our belongings, so the driver can be on his way." Aud moved toward the baggage box and started to help with the luggage.

"I told you I'd do that, Aud." Turk stepped in front of her and nearly dropped the large valise the driver thrust at him.

Audrey grabbed the next trunk and manhandled it as if it contained feathers.

"Audrey, Audrey, Audrey." Sayra grabbed her friend's hand. "Just let him push them up against the station house for now. No one will steal them, and I'll send my landlady's son over to fetch them for us later. Let's get to the church so all of you get a chance to visit with Shago and Tru a little while before the ceremony. I'd like to introduce you to Brother Caleb, our minister, then show you where you can freshen up."

Dusting her hands, Aud nodded. "Well, why not? I guess stepping foot inside a church with four walls ought to be one of those new experiences I planned on having this trip."

Bess's shocked look inspired a laugh from Sayra. "Don't worry, Sis. She's one of the most God-fearing people I know. I'll explain it all to you later."

Sayra grabbed her sister's arm and led the Van Burens and the two miners toward the church. It took every ounce of willpower not to run—for pure joy this time—toward the destiny God had planned for her, instead of away from it.

❧

Bess opened the door of the telegraph office and stuck her head around the edge. "Ready?"

Sayra nodded, then took a moment to look one more time at the place where she'd first heard Truman's confession of love. The office was closer to the church and had been chosen as the place where she would wait to become his bride. And wait she had for the long years after her parents' death, through the often difficult times of living under Ulysses' roof, until now when God in

His great wisdom guided her straight into Truman's arms. The next time she walked into this room, it would be as Mrs. Truman Taylor. Telegrapher. Helpmate. Wife.

"Come on, Sis. Lily's getting anxious."

"Nervous jitters?"

"Chattering so fast, I can't get a word in edgewise. You know how she gets when she's excited."

"And Shago, how's he holding up?" Sayra asked.

Respect shone in Bess's eyes. "Like the champion he is. He looks like a pine towering over her, standing so straight and tall. But it's the strength of love in his eyes for sweet Lily that makes me proud. Oh, Sayra, we'd prayed all this for her, didn't we?"

"And I'd say heaven heard us." Sayra hugged her sister, careful not to wrinkle the delicate lace cascading in ruffles over her white satin wedding dress.

"You look beautiful, Sayra."

"Thanks, Bess. Let's hope Truman feels the same."

Instead of the anticipated nervousness Sayra thought she would feel upon approaching the church, a calm unlike anything she'd ever known settled over her. She greeted her niece at the door as Bess slipped quietly inside to signal Brother Caleb all was ready.

Teresa Clark and Karen Kay, sisters who tried to rival each other in hitting the highest note, began to sing. Hearing the cue, Lily started the walk down the aisle, followed immediately by Sayra.

Though Sayra felt every eye focus first on Lily, then on herself, she saw only one pair. Truman's emerald eyes, shining with love and commitment, gazed at her and promised eternity.

Ulysses joined Lily and escorted her to where Shago stood, trembling yet stronger than he'd ever been. Aud stood beside Lily as maid-of-honor. Turk joined Sayra, presenting her in marriage to Truman as her father would have, if he'd lived to see this day. She thanked Turk and handed her bouquet to Bess, whom she'd chosen as matron-of-honor.

"So beautiful."

Her heart leapt with joy stirred by Tru's whispered reverence as she took her place beside him. The black suit and string tie was his Sunday best, but it was his rugged good looks and bronzed face that stole her breath away.

"Dearly Beloved, we are gathered here today in the sight of God. . . ," the ageless ceremony began.

Sayra listened to every word, freely accepting each commitment, promising to love him beyond a time that death might part them and vowing she would never forget the blessing she'd been given this day. . . Truman's love.

And when at last the final "I do" was said and Brother Caleb announced, "You may now kiss your brides," Lily shouted a loud, "Aaaaaamen!"

Shago grinned and lifted her veil to accommodate his bride.

Sayra faced Tru. "When do I get that spectacular kiss you promised a while back?"

Truman exhaled a pent-up breath. "You mean an eternity ago, don't you? This was the longest month of my life." His eyes warmed to a smoky green. "Yes, my darling, you get that kiss. . .but only on one condition."

"And what is that, my love?" she whispered softly,

her breath mingling with his.

"That you promise to love me forever. The only place I ever want you running is straight into my arms."

She answered him with a kiss. He'd captured her heart with a simple game of truth; she'd won his love by sharing faith. Every day for the rest of her life, Sayra would count the blessings that had, indeed, led her to Truman.

"Say, preacher," Turk cleared his throat when the couples took longer than he felt comfortable with sealing their vows.

"Yes, Brother Turkelrod?"

"You wouldn't feel like marrying up another somebody or two, would you?"

Aud Williams craned her neck around Lily and Shago. "What put such a fool notion into that head of yours?"

A skunk-eating grin spread across the prospector's face. "Well, I figure it would make spending the winter holed up with you a mite more interesting this year."

For the second time since Sayra had met the miner, Aud Williams blushed scarlet to the tips of her ears.

A Letter To Our Readers

Dear Reader:

In order that we might better contribute to your reading enjoyment, we would appreciate your taking a few minutes to respond to the following questions. When completed, please return to the following:

Rebecca Germany, Managing Editor
Heartsong Presents
P.O. Box 719
Uhrichsville, Ohio 44683

1. Did you enjoy reading *Small Blessings*?
   ❑ Very much. I would like to see more books
   by this author!
   ❑ Moderately
   I would have enjoyed it more if _____

   _____

2. Are you a member of **Heartsong Presents**? ❑Yes ❑No
   If no, where did you purchase this book?_____

   _____

3. What influenced your decision to purchase this
   book? (Check those that apply.)

   ❑ Cover   ❑ Back cover copy

   ❑ Title   ❑ Friends

   ❑ Publicity   ❑ Other_____

4. How would you rate, on a scale from 1 (poor) to 5
   (superior), the cover design?_____

5. On a scale from 1 (poor) to 10 (superior), please rate the following elements.

       ___-Heroine   ___Plot

       ___ Hero   ___ Inspirational theme

       ___ Setting   ___Secondary characters

6. What settings would you like to see covered in **Heartsong Presents** books?_____

_____

_____

7. What are some inspirational themes you would like to see treated in future books?_____

_____

_____

8. Would you be interested in reading other **Heartsong Presents** titles?   ❏ Yes   ❏ No

9. Please check your age range:
   ❏ Under 18   ❏ 18-24   ❏ 25-34
   ❏ 35-45   ❏ 46-55   ❏ Over 55

10. How many hours per week do you read? _____

Name _____

Occupation _____

Address _____

City_____ State_____ Zip _____

Comfort
FOOD

Ellen W. Caughey

Welcome to the kitchen of *Comfort Food*, a warm inviting space where tantalizing aromas mingle with the sage advice of Scripture, where low-fat foods are not a mélange of mysterious ingredients, where pride of family recipes is as fulfilling as the looks of satisfaction after a relished repast.

Welcome to a hearty collection of soups, main dishes, and desserts that stand ready to satisfy every comfort-seeking appetite. Includes 29 recipes that will make you feel right at home. 64 pages, Hardbound, 5" x 6 ½"

·····Hearts♥ng·····

HEARTSONG PRESENTS TITLES AVAILABLE NOW:

·········Presents·········

Great Inspirational Romance at a Great Price!

Heartsong Presents books are inspirational romances in contemporary and historical settings, designed to give you an enjoyable, spirit-lifting reading experience. You can choose wonderfully written titles from some of today's best authors like Peggy Darty, Colleen L. Reece, Tracie J. Peterson, VeraLee Wiggins, and many others.

When ordering quantities less than twelve, above titles are $2.95 each.